The Veiled

The Shilund Saga Book 1

Jennifer Osborn

Indescribable
Publishing

For Bill, you make me a better woman.

Prologue

Late August

"Get the lead out. I'd like to make it to a good spot before it gets dark. From the looks of it, we don't have long," Jack Day yelled over his shoulder to his two closest friends, Chris Jenkins and Adam Hensley, annoyed at the situation.

The men carried heavy packs as they moved along the uneven ground, miles into the dense woods of Presque Isle, Maine. All three were rookie firefighters. It was the first night in months they'd had off together, and they'd decided to celebrate with a camping trip. Where guys their age usually had two or more years left of college, they were already beginning the probationary period in their chosen occupation.

All had military-style haircuts and muscular builds, though Jack stood taller than the other two, with coffee-colored hair and icy-blue eyes. Chris had coal-black hair with eyes so brown you could hardly see the pupils. The last of the three, Adam, seemed to fit more with the California surfer types – flaxen hair and ocean-water blue eyes.

The sun had just retreated behind the hill line beyond them and the sky had dimmed, hints of fuchsia, gold, and amber ushering out the retreating light.

"Yeah, yeah, yeah," Chris complained, directly behind Jack. "It was your idea to go this deep into the woods in the first place, Day. I have no idea why you want to primitive camp anyway. I would have camped by our car if it were left up to me."

Jack turned and glared at Chris and opened his mouth to speak right as Adam reached forward and flicked Chris in the ear. "Whiner."

Chris stopped walking. He froze like he wanted to wheel around and punch Adam in the chest. Instead, he replied, "Do that again, and I'll show you what real whining is all about." He took a few steps before another flick hit his ear.

Abruptly, he spun around to catch Adam, but Adam was already running away, his blond head jolting up and down as he tried to escape, hefting his heavy pack across the clumpy ground littered with branches and downed trees.

Chris chased him while attempting to balance his own large

backpack, but it proved too difficult. He toppled to the ground, landing so hard that a strong gust of air left his lungs in a burst.

Jack and Adam's laughter echoed off the trees. Chris appeared to stifle a comment as he unhooked his pack from his waist and tried to wiggle his arms free of the tight straps, but the snug pack resisted and held him firmly in place.

"Easy as taking candy from a baby. He looks like a turtle knocked over on its shell," Adam mocked as he gazed over Chris with his hands on his knees. Jack laughed and offered a hand to help Chris up.

"No, thank you," Chris shot back before he eventually worked himself free of his pack and made it to his feet.

"How is it that you can carry one hundred and ten pounds of hose up five stories without losing your breath, and you can't balance a thirty-five-pound bag on your shoulders?" Jack challenged as he took off his own pack, dropping it with a thud into the tall grass.

Chris shot Jack an irritated look, but he didn't reply. Instead, he glanced around. "How about here, Jack? Looks good enough to me."

They scanned the area from where they stood at the edge of a small, grassy clearing, lined by lumbering tupelos, maples, and basswood trees. In between were skinny pines, reaching high up into the sky.

Jack nodded. "Okay. If it will keep the both of you from complaining."

"Nah, he'll still whine," Adam said as he ran by Chris, flicking him once more on the ear.

Chris gave chase since he was free to run this time, disappearing into the brush after his friend. Adam's taunts about Chris' manhood echoed, and Jack could hear their scuffling, realizing Chris had finally caught Adam.

Chris broke through the tree line, dragging Adam back in a headlock. Adam struggled, but Chris' hold was firm.

"Where do you want this trash?" Chris asked innocently, managing to restrain a squirming Adam with his arm.

They were always punching each other, playing practical jokes, and making each other's lives challenging. Ignoring them, Jack shook his head and began unloading his pack, smiling.

* * *

"Too bad Henry couldn't make it," Jack said as he reclined against a log and watched the dancing fire while it crackled and popped. He took a drink of his beer and then tossed a pinecone into the blaze. The crickets lulled him into contentment with their rhythmic song, and the air had just settled into a cooler temperature. Things couldn't be any better for Jack.

"What was up with that, anyway?" Adam asked. "He looked like he'd sucked on a lemon when you asked him." He stared up into the clear night sky, a look of awe crossing his face. The stars were pinholes against a black blanket. "Why would he want to miss this?"

"I don't know. He said he had stuff to do. I think Sheriff Pike had him working on something." Jack shrugged.

"Probably wants to organize the property locker in the sheriff's office alphabetically." Chris chuckled. "Does he realize he has OCD?"

"Henry's not OCD," Jack retorted. "Just...organized."

Chris gave him a droll stare. "He probably has his closet arranged by color."

Jack couldn't help it; he laughed. Henry was the fourth member of this motley posse. Where Chris, Adam, and Jack were firefighters, Henry was a deputy, and they were all inseparable. They hung out every free moment they had and almost always at Jack's house.

Adam sat up. "He's probably like the crazy freak in that Julia Roberts movie. What was it called?"

"You watch Julia Roberts movies?" Jack snorted.

Adam's eyebrow rose. "Well, once. My sister made me," he said defensively. "But that's not the point."

"*Pretty Woman*?" Chris guessed.

Jack shot Chris a surprised look. Chris shrugged.

"No, that wasn't it. You know, the crazy husband that likes his labels turned out on his canned food."

Jack laughed. "*Sleeping with the Enemy*?"

Adam perked up, the fire reflecting off his hair. He waved his hands around dramatically. "Yeah, that's it. He's probably like that crazy husband, playing freaky classical music and rearranging his towels so they line up."

Jack threw an empty bottle at Adam while stifling a laugh. The bottle hit his shin. "Stop! He's nothing like that. At least he keeps his stuff organized. When was the last time you mustered on a practice run and had everything together? Chief Merchant is going to have your butt in a sling if you don't stop misplacing stuff."

"*Ow*," Adam complained and rubbed his leg. "I know where everything is. I just use a different organizational method than most."

He smiled and glanced up again, regarding the sky.

Jack's gaze followed Adam's, and he studied the expanse above him. It was so dark and clear here. So dark that millions of stars were visible, strewn across the expanse. The only variation was the sliver of the moon hanging low. In an odd way, Jack could truly breathe here. All the worries of work and life washed away in beer and laughter, far away from everything.

A strange, wet thud from Chris' direction caught Jack's attention. It took a moment for him to figure out what he was looking at.

Blood ran from Chris' mouth in a flood. His lips gaped like a fish out of water. He reached up slowly to a spear protruding ten inches out of his chest, lightly touching it like he was trying to figure out what it was and how it got there. Then as Chris' confused eyes bore into Jack's, he slumped over.

A rush of wind came from his left, and when Jack jerked his head around, he caught a glimpse of Adam's kicking legs as they disappeared into the brush, an anguished cry bellowing out.

Jack jumped up, and pain lanced his side. He started to look down, but fell backward over the log. A flash of green appeared before his eyes, and then everything went black.

Chapter 1: The meeting

Miles outside of Presque Isle, deep in the woods in the middle of the blackest night of a new moon, a lone figure shrouded in a flowing, black robe moved along the uneven land of the forest floor. Breaking through the edge of the woodland into a small, open space, the specter pulled a travois of large tree branches, upon which lay the body of an unconscious man. The man's body bounced as he was pulled over rocks and tree roots, but he never woke. He merely bobbed with the movement of the makeshift stretcher.

The cloaked form arrived at a cabin, nestled in the thickest part of the unexplored forest. Without effort, it easily shrugged the man onto its shoulders and stepped inside.

The dwelling was warm, illuminated by the raging blaze in the fireplace. The being lay the man down on a bed and rearranged his limbs into a more comfortable position. It reached down again to lay his arms over his stomach before returning them to the original position, on either side of his body. Seemingly satisfied, it moved away and sat at the far end of the small room to wait.

The fire hissed as a log collapsed down onto the others in the fireplace. The figure in the chair adjusted the sleeves of the robe it wore, pulling them down over its hands.

* * *

Jack moaned and opened his eyes, blinking repeatedly. His brows furrowed, his gaze darting around frantically. Then he spotted the statue-still person in the corner.

"Where am I?" he grunted.

No answer came.

"Please." He attempted to rise on his elbows, but he winced in pain. Letting his body back down, he panted and turned again to the corner. "Where am I?"

The figure shifted slightly, and a small, feminine voice answered, "At my home."

"What? Your home? Where—wait...how did I get here?" The question sounded strained as he attempted to rise, but then he collapsed, groaning. "Where are Chris and Adam?"

"You need to relax," she suggested softly. "You've been badly wounded, and you're bleeding."

Her voice was so melodic to Jack that he calmed down and took in deep breaths to get through the ripping pain in his side. He reached down, his fingers brushing over a thick bandage. Lifting the blood-soaked covering, he forced his head up off the bed and could see a ragged tear in his side, oozing a steady stream of blood. Covering it back over, he knew he needed to keep pressure on it to slow the bleeding, but doing that was more difficult than it sounded. The pain was intense, almost to the point of passing out.

He wondered where he was and with whom. Glancing around the one-room cabin, he found it was almost stark, having just a table, chair, and bed. The only light came from the fire, casting a strange glow over everything. It seemed utterly surreal.

"What happened to me? One minute, I was with my friends, and then something happened. I can't remember. Did I have an accident?"

"You could say that," she replied, thick with sarcasm. Jack noticed her feet shift underneath the fabric of her cloak.

He scrubbed his hand over his scruffy chin and tried to remember the last thing he'd been doing. He was camping with his friends and had just settled around the fire to drink beer, when...when...God, it was so hard to remember.

Green, he thought. *There was a flash of green.*

Why couldn't he remember anything but that? It was like falling in a dream, spiraling downward in a nauseating twirl.

"I was camping with Chris and Adam...I saw something green, and that's all I can remember. Where are they? Are they okay?" He turned his face again to the silhouette in the corner.

"You don't need to know that now. It wouldn't ease your mind any," her angelic voice replied.

"What? Of course I need to know. Are they okay?" he demanded.

"No, you don't. Trust me." The figure's legs shifted again.

He grew impatient by her shrouded appearance. "Can you come out where I can see you?" he begged.

"It's best if I don't. Now, you need to be quiet and rest. I don't want to talk about what happened earlier. So stop asking."

He could tell she was frustrated and hesitant, and he immediately tensed. "Please. What happened to my friends? Do they know where I am?"

The silence was heavy, and it only aggravated him more.

Abruptly, she asked, "What do they call you?"

"Do you mean my name?"

"Yes."

"My name is Jackson Day. And you still didn't answer me. I want to know what happened to my friends. Please."

She spoke slowly, "Well, Jackson Day, your friends…Adam and Chris…are dead."

It was as if all the air left the room and everything was spinning on its side. *This isn't real. This has to be a bad dream*, he thought. *She didn't just say they were dead, did she?* That wasn't right. They weren't dead. They couldn't be.

"I don't understand. We were camping, drinking beer..." Jack clarified, his voice trailing off.

"Enough," she growled. "No more questions, Jackson Day. I will not discuss it further."

His mind began to turn everything over. Flashes of memories rushed through his head in quick succession, but never led to answers. This was probably how Alice felt when she fell down the rabbit hole. But he wasn't Alice, and this wasn't a journey to Wonderland. No, he was in a nightmare with a strange woman from whom he physically was incapable of escaping.

"Can I call someone?" Jack asked tightly, staring at her dark figure sitting across the room.

"Call someone? No. I don't have a phone, Jackson Day. Even if I did, I couldn't let you call anyone. For now, it is just you and I. And please, try to rest. You won't heal otherwise."

Her voice had a strange tone. Was it pleading? Concern? Exasperation? He couldn't tell. He laid his head back and closed his eyes.

"No, no, no," he whispered, shaking his head. He had to get out, now. He needed to find Chris and Adam and get them some help. They weren't dead—that was impossible. They might be injured somewhere, just like he was, and he needed to get to them and find some help.

Jack tried to push himself up with his arms so he could get out of bed, only to pass out from the pain.

Chapter 2: Jack

Jack awoke to the sound of shifting fabric and footsteps. He forced his eyes open and stared up at an unfinished, wooden-beamed roof, trying to figure out where he was. Dull light poured in from the bare windows, so he figured it was morning. He angled his head and spotted a woman moving around the table; her thick, raven hair fell forward, completely obscuring her face. She was rapidly slicing bread.

Parts of the prior night came rushing back. She'd brought him here, somehow, after he had been hurt. His head was foggy, and he couldn't bring order to all of the flashes of memory bouncing around in his mind like bullets.

Her hands caught his attention. They were so creamy and smooth, like a porcelain doll. It made him want to see the rest of her. Her tall, trim frame exuded an aura of strength and power. She wore black, threadbare canvas pants and a black sweater with a hole in the side, revealing milky white skin underneath.

Look at me, he thought. He wanted to know if the rest of her was as perfect as her hands.

Immediately, she turned to stare at him. He involuntarily gasped. She had a pale, angular face with a slightly pointed chin. But it was her eyes that held his attention. The irises were a bright, glowing amber—the pupils oblong like a cat's. Peeking out from under her lips were the tips of two canines, longer than the rest of her teeth. He couldn't help but wonder what had happened to her to deform her eyes and teeth like that.

Instinct told him to retreat, and he inched closer to the wall at his side, not knowing whether or not she intended him harm, but he was immobile and couldn't get away from her. Holding up his arms, he yelled, "What are you?"

She glared at him, curled her lip back, and hissed. "I am what you humans should be afraid of!" she growled, menacingly, and hurled the knife at the wall. It embedded itself a few feet from the bed with a thud and reverberated from the force. The woman whirled around and deftly went out the front door, slamming it hard behind her.

You humans?

Jack panted in fear and pain, all senses on high alert. What was she if she wasn't human? She had features like a cat, but the rest of her appeared normal. Warning bells in his head told him he was in danger and needed to get away.

When he tried to sit up, debilitating pain shot through his chest in protest. Lying back, he tried to slow down his breathing and come up with a plan for getting away. He had to devise a plan for escaping. He needed to find Chris and Adam.

Glancing over to the knife embedded in the wall, he tried to scoot to reach it, but his fingers couldn't bridge the distance. Moving again, he pushed through the hot, stabbing agony and grabbed for the handle, but it was useless. It may have only been three feet away, but in his physical state, it might as well have been three hundred. After gritting his teeth and attempting it again, he almost passed out from the effort. He had to stop, not wanting to be unconscious around her if he could help it.

He stared up at the ceiling, realizing he was trapped for the moment, and hoping he could garner enough goodwill from the woman that she would spare his life.

Who was he kidding? He was at her mercy and he knew it, awake or unconscious.

Admittedly, she hadn't hurt him so far, so that was a good sign. He tried not to think about the fact that she had hurled the knife at his head. He prayed she had meant to miss him.

To reassure himself, he replayed the events of last night, bent on remembering what had happened. He could recall the hike, setting up the camp, and the millions of stars at night.

Then?

An image of Chris with blood running down his chin flashed in his mind.

Jack's heart thudded hard. That was right. The last time he'd seen Chris, his friend had a spear jutting out of his chest.

Panic set in, and his heart beat even faster.

Something had pulled Adam into the brush, too. Had some wild animal attacked them? No, animals didn't carry spears. That meant it had to have been an attack by people. But why? Why? It didn't make any sense. Who would attack them?

A warning that an eccentric old man had given him right before they left to go camping echoed in his head, "*It's dangerous to go too far into the woods. Some people never come back out.*"

He didn't want to believe Adam and Chris were dead. They were good men. Tears pricked his eyes, and his chest tightened as if it turned inside out. He only hoped that, if they were dead, it had been quick and painless. More than that, he needed to know how they died, and by God, the woman would answer him.

What if *she'd* killed them? What if she was going to let him lie here and bleed to death? Could it have been her? Could she have been that evil to kill his best friends?

Steeling his determination, he knew he had to prepare to fight if need be. He would not remain some hapless victim, just to be killed by this woman. He might be weak and most definitely hurt, but he'd die with dignity, fighting the whole way.

* * *

He realized he had fallen asleep when the woman returned and jarred him awake. The light had changed positions in the window, so he knew a few hours had passed. She stood just inside the door, almost like she contemplated going back out again. But she eventually shut it and stopped at the table, gazing wide-eyed at Jack.

Her eyes seemed to hypnotize him, and he could do nothing but stare at her, the gold in them almost glowing.

"Are you hungry?" she asked softly.

"Hungry?" If she was going to kill him, why did it matter if he was hungry or not?

She chuckled. "You are not too bright, are you? You know, in need of sustenance? Food?" She made a scooping motion with her hand toward her mouth.

He was hungry, but was this a trick? Should he take anything she offered? He couldn't decide. Maybe she wanted to watch him writhe in pain from something she fed him.

"Are you going to poison me?" His eyes would not leave her, and he detected a little annoyance.

"Poison you? You think I mean you harm?" She sighed and sat down in the chair now resting between the bed and the table. "It's to be expected, I suppose. You sense danger and are fearful. I suppose my outburst only helped solidify that." She rubbed her forehead. "Well, you have a right to be afraid of my kind. But I'll tell you this, Jackson Day, I mean you no harm. You have my word."

She reached for the discarded bread lying on the table. She stood, approached him slowly, and held the bread just within his reach but no closer. He shook his head.

Sighing, she tore off a chunk and ate it in demonstration. Thrusting it back at him, she raised her eyebrows.

Reluctantly, Jack took the bread and nodded. "Thank you." He bit off a piece, chewing mechanically just to get it down.

Gracefully, she stepped to the counter beyond the table, her movements almost cat-like. She poured something into a cup and returned. She held the cup out, again standing close enough for him to reach it but not her.

As thirsty as he was, he couldn't sit up. It was too painful to move his body into a position that would keep him from spilling it all over him. He finally gave up and let his hand hold the cup at his side.

With a troubled expression, she folded her arms across her chest and watched him. Like a guardian angel. A menacing, scary, guardian angel.

"You know, it's not fair you know my name, but I don't know yours."

She sat back down in her chair and said nothing for what seemed like an eternity. "They call me Serena."

It's a pretty name, Jack thought. "Nice to meet you, Serena."

Serena only nodded, while continuing to watch him eat the bread. Abruptly, she got up and stood over him. She seemed tentative.

Jack stiffened and stopped eating, expecting her to hurt him. He grasped the cup hard, preparing to hurl it at her, when, without warning, she pulled it from his hand in the quickest move he'd ever witnessed.

"If you are going to kill me, I warn you, I won't go down without a fight," he huffed.

Serena pulled back and her eyebrows shot up. Slowly, a smile crept across her face, exposing her pearly white teeth and sharp fangs. "If I wanted you dead, Jackson Day, you'd be dead. I just want to help you get a drink. It's painful to watch you struggle. Let me help."

This stopped Jack short. He'd expected anything but that. He gave permission with a slight nod.

She smelled like fresh air and sweet pine. It was the most comforting scent. She gently placed her arm under his torso and lifted him to take a good sip. He groaned as his body was moved, but he tried to suppress it so he could drink.

The cool liquid had a minty taste, and it quenched his thirst. He found himself gripping her hand as she held the cup. He couldn't get it down fast enough.

"Slowly, Jackson Day, or you will choke."

Jack wasn't listening; he simply drank it until nothing was left. She helped him lie back on the bed again and as she turned away, he grabbed her arm.

She stared apprehensively at his hand.

"Thank you, Serena."

Serena smiled, and it hit Jack how beautiful she was, despite her strange eyes and fangs. His gaze stayed locked on her face for what seemed like years.

He made himself release her arm, but she made no move to turn away. She watched him with curiosity.

She is beautiful, odd eyes, sharp teeth, and all.

"Please rest, Jackson Day."

"Jack."

She frowned. "Jack?"

He nodded as he closed his eyes. "Yes, either Jackson or Jack, I'll answer to both, but you don't need to keep using my full name."

"Full name?" she questioned. "What is a full name?"

"You know, your first name is Serena. My first name is Jack," he explained, his eyes still closed. "My last name is Day. So either Jack or Jackson. I don't really care to be called 'Day,' which is what most call me at the firehouse. Everyone there uses last names and I can't get them to break the habit for me. Speaking of, do you have a last name?" He peered up at her.

She stared blankly at him for a moment. "No. I don't have a last name."

"No last name? How can that be?" He moved and winced as pain shot up through him like an electrical shock. He paused and took in a breath.

"Jack. Please rest. You need to heal. We can talk later." Her gaze, those wide, glowing amber eyes, held the most determined expression.

"Yeah, okay," he ground out and let his eyes slip closed.

He could tell that she had moved away from him, but then she didn't make any more noise. The pain was intense and all he could focus on. So, he tried to just think about what was around him. Little by little, the crackling of the fire and the birds chirping outside relaxed him. He found he no longer could lift his arms or legs, but it didn't seem to matter as he slowly drifted off to sleep.

Chapter 3: **Serena**

Serena stood over Jack as he lay on her small bed. His body was too large for it and his limbs hung off the edge. She sat beside him, leaning in close to stare at his face, resisting the urge to feel his skin against her fingertips.

His features were truly becoming, even more so than males of her kind. His hair was the color of silhouetted trees at dusk; so brown it was almost black. His lean face had a strong jaw and was in need of a shave. His thick, dark lashes stood out against his tan face and when his eyes were open, the blue of them reminded her of a cloudless summer day.

She snapped a couple of times by his ear to see if he'd react, but he didn't stir. The herbs must have taken effect. This way, she could attend to him without inflicting pain. She had been fighting her panic the entire time, hoping the bleeding would slow so he didn't bleed to death before she had a chance to sew the wound in his side.

He was lucky he was still alive. Serena shivered. Had she been just a minute later, he would have been dead. Her only regret was that she couldn't save his friends. For a slight moment, she hated what she was. Her kind had done this to him and it was the worst sort of depravity.

She took off his shoes and socks, letting them drop unceremoniously to the floor. Tapping her fingers on her thigh, she knew she was stalling. She still needed to get his shirt and pants off. She'd just be as careful as possible while taking care of him and try not to look where she shouldn't.

Slowly, she started to remove his pants. What would Rahfey, as well as the others, think of her touching a male, and a human at that? The others would condemn her, and she would forever be undesirable in the eyes of the clan. But, no worry, she had adjusted to the forced isolation, so what would it matter if she were forever shunned? The only other thing they could do to her was kill her and that didn't scare her in the slightest.

After gently pulling his pants off, she was about to toss them on the floor but paused to look at them. They were so dirty and bloody. She would try to wash them so that he'd have something clean.

Gazing at him, she thought his legs were lovely—tanned, muscular, and perfectly proportioned. His thighs were strong and powerful, as if he was used to running or working hard. She wanted to touch the hair at his calves and shins. Before she realized what she was doing, she was reaching out to do so.

This is not proper. You are an unmated female and he is a male, she argued with herself, her body refusing to do what her mind told her.

Her fingertips softly brushed the hair, and it tickled. Her lips lifted in surprise at its softness. A purr was rising in her throat, but she forced it to stop. Coming to her senses, she pulled back her hands. She needed to focus and to complete her clinical mission of undressing him so she could tend to his wound.

It was the work of the moment to get him out of his ripped shirt. He now lay only in his underwear, dirt and blood caking his body. She was surprised by how handsome she found this human. He was defined and lean, cut in flawless lines, more perfect than any other human or Shilund she had ever seen. As she regarded him, emotions churned in her stomach.

Focus, Serena, focus.

With a bowl of water, along with a cloth and soap, she started to bathe him, taking care to wipe away the grime and blood stuck to his body. She found the purring building again, but this time, she allowed it. There was no one to tell her she couldn't.

She gently wiped down his arms and hands, stopping every so often just to look at him, his skin glistening in the shimmering firelight. Serena was fascinated about every part of him and realized that humans were not so different from her kind. They were identical in almost every way.

She turned to the table, grabbing some alcohol, a needle, and thread. Thank God her friend Vivienne had given her these things. What would she have done without her? She was her only true friend in the world.

After a time, she finished applying ointment to the various scratches and cuts and wrapped a bandage around his side. As she stood, she smiled, feeling rather accomplished at having tended his wounds. It was a small act of redemption to save him. But there was something else growing inside of her, an attraction that she tried to tap down. But it made her feel alive, as wrong as it was.

She pulled the chair nearer to the bed and sat there, studying his face, allowing her fingertips to trail over his eyes, nose, and lips. If she were sane, she would keep trying to scare him off, so that when he was healed and left, he would not return.

This sent a pang of regret through her. She wanted so much for him to like her, to accept her and be her friend. But that was impossible. No matter what, it just couldn't happen. He had been attacked by her kind and that was certainly a detail he would probably not be able to get past.

Standing up, she knew it would be a while before he was conscious. She needed to see if she could make contact with her friend. She banked the fire and then went back to him. Drawing a blanket up over him, she took one last look at him before disappearing out the door.

Chapter 4: Jack

When Jack awoke, he was quick to realize where he was. He brushed his arm over his chest and found his shirt was gone. Looking underneath the blanket now covering him, he discovered he was only in his underwear, cleaned and re-bandaged. Heat rushed into his cheeks.

Oh God, she undressed me.

Sunshine poured in through the two windows on the front of the cabin, cascading down into pillars of light as the dust danced in its brightness. Birds chirped happily outside. It was surreal to think he was the survivor of an attack that had killed his best friends.

He searched the room for Serena, but she wasn't there. This both disappointed and relieved him. He wanted to talk to her again, try to get some answers now that his mind was less cloudy. Maybe with her gone, he could try to get up.

He remembered the knife stuck in the wall. Looking over, he saw it was gone and his heart sank.

Damn.

He forced himself up, gritting his teeth through the pain. Sitting up gave him a false sense of having some control over the situation. Who was he kidding? He wasn't going to be getting out of this bed today. His heart sank. He didn't like being this helpless, but there was absolutely nothing he could do about it.

Leaning his head against the wall, he was thankful his thoughts seemed clearer. Nothing like almost being killed to fog up your brain. It wasn't like him to just sit and do nothing about this or any other situation he had found himself in. His mother always called him a doer, and he needed to get that part of him to wake up and figure this out.

Looking around the cabin, he was surprised at how clean and sparse of personal items it was. And where had she been sleeping? There wasn't another bed. This small cabin did not look like a home. It was stark and cold, not like a place someone lived in. Serena had nothing here that claimed the space as hers. No keepsakes, no items beyond a few books. It was so odd.

Serena was such an enigma, and he found himself curious to know every detail about her. And why had she brought him here? She could have called the park rangers to take him to a hospital, but that hadn't happened. Why? What happened after all? What killed his friends and almost killed him? Try as he might, he couldn't connect all the dots of that night.

Chris had been impaled by something. He remembered a flash of green. Then nothing. Why couldn't he remember?

His sense of time seemed skewed too. How long ago had that been? Two days, a week? Everything seemed to blend into this fevered dream.

The door opened with a creak and Serena stood there holding an armful of firewood, a slight flush to her cheeks.

"Good, you are awake." Serena dropped the wood by the fire. "How are you feeling?" She stared at him with those odd cat eyes and he wanted to squirm.

"Better. A little clearer."

Both of them remained still in the quiet. Jack wasn't sure what else she wanted, but she seemed expectant.

"Do you have anything more to eat?" He absentmindedly rubbed at his bare stomach.

Serena's gaze flickered down to the movement of his hand before jerking back up to his eyes.

"I only have the bread for the moment, but I will find a way to get human food more to your liking. I will leave shortly to get it."

Human? What was she?

"The bread would be great," he allowed.

She gave him a small nod and walked to the counter, her thick, raven hair swinging down her back. There were slight waves in it, and it appeared luminous as it caught the light. He wanted to touch it to see if it was as soft as it seemed.

"You have beautiful hair. Has anyone told you that?"

Serena turned slowly, walking to him with her face down. She tentatively handed him the bread. Her reply was soft. "That's not something our kind says. So, no." Serena turned and grabbed a cup of water, offering it to him, her gold eyes blazing.

Taking a drink, he watched her as she sat down across the room.

She must have moved the chair away from me.

"Thank you." He wanted her a little closer. When she sat so far away it was like a buffer between them. He should probably want that, shouldn't he?

Again, Serena only nodded, staring as he ate what was left of the bread in two bites and drank down the water. Once he finished both, she stood and took the cup from his hand.

"You need your rest, Jack. Lie down."

He had to admit his energy waned, and sweat had spread across his forehead from the effort of eating that small amount. Internally, he warred with wanting rest and needing answers. So, figuring the easiest way to get both was to comply, he started the slow process of moving through the pain, only to have Serena's warm hands helping him lay back. Jack gazed up at her and grinned his thanks. Serena averted her eyes and quickly moved away.

"Serena. I hope you don't mind, but I have a lot of questions. Please, will you answer some for me?"

She dropped her weight into the chair and sighed loudly in annoyance. "What do you want to know?" she said, surrendering. "I'll tell you what I can. But there may be some things I cannot answer."

"Okay." He shifted the pillow behind his head. "First, why did you call me human? Aren't we both? Are you like in a weird religious cult where you renounce your humanity?"

Serena studied her hands and then met his gaze head on. "No. I'm not human. I am what your Native Americans called 'Night People.' My people are ancient and live hidden from the human world. I do not know what a religious cult is."

"Forgive me, but I still don't understand. So, like I asked before, what else is there? If you are not human, what are you?"

An internal struggle played out on her face. "My people are called Shilund," she slowly explained. "We are not human; we're our own kind. Kind of like how a wolf is different from a boar. Both have arms, legs, and a mouth, so do we, just like you humans. But just as the wolf and boar, we are not the same.

"Humans used to live side by side with us, but somewhere, something changed, and fear crept in, causing dissension between Shilunds and humans. We learned to hide, and now we've become..." She seemed to search for words. "What you humans call 'boogiemen' and the stuff of folk tales to scare your children. Many human stories of things creeping in the night have their origin with the Shilund. But, since humans never carry history accurately from generation to generation, they have forgotten we are real and relegated us to mere inaccurate legend. In some ways, that keeps us safe, so that suits us."

Jack frowned. "Where did the Shilund come from? I mean, we

must have the same origins since we are so similar, as you pointed out."

A small grin crept over Serena's face briefly and then disappeared. "I know not where we came from. We just are. As far as being like you, I don't know. I've never been around humans... except—" She paused. "I think we're like humans in some ways, different in others." She turned away from him.

"How are we different?" Jack asked. "Aside from the obvious physical differences?"

Serena gave a small chuckle, seemingly enjoying the conversation. She gazed directly at him, her chest rising as she sucked in a deep breath.. "We are stronger than you physically, and we have heightened senses. We can see in total darkness as well. But beyond that and how we look, I'm not sure how we are different. My people do hate humans and have been known to kill them for sport."

The blood drained from Jack's face.

"Have you killed for sport?" He immediately thought of his dead friends, and his voice grew louder. "Did you kill my friends for sport?"

He struggled to get out of bed and fell to the ground right as Serena reached him. Feeling panicked and angry, he tried to push her away, although it did little to impede her.

"Get away from me!" he yelled, falling back on his arms, excruciating pain radiating from his side. He fought to stay conscious through the agony. Part of his brain said if he passed out, his number might be up.

"Please, you will hurt yourself! Let me help you!" Serena struggled to get a hold of Jack, all the while his arms batting her away.

"Is that what you did? You killed my friends?" Jack accused.

An injured look flitted across her face, and she dropped her arms. "No!" Serena growled, her expression incredulous. "I've never hurt a human! Never!"

Jack scrambled away, inching closer to the wall. "Whatever. I don't believe you. They're dead! Someone killed them."

Serena's liquid gold eyes bore into his, her features a mask of disbelief, her tone unemotional. "If I killed humans, you'd be dead. No question. Dead. Instead, I brought you here, to protect you."

"Leave me alone," he bellowed through gritted teeth, grasping his side. He wanted to get away from her, from this place, from this complete and total nightmare. How could he sit here and casually have this conversation with a woman, or whatever she was, like it was a

Sunday lunch. Adam and Chris were dead, and she might have killed them.

She didn't kill you. Maybe you're wrong about her, he thought in the midst of his temper.

Serena rose to her full height, towering over him, her eyes wounded. She was so close he could smell sweet evergreen. After a few tense moments, she pursed her lips then ran from the cabin and slammed the door.

Jack sat panting, angry and aching. He wanted answers and there was this odd sensation that she was holding something meaningful back. Seeing her react like she had, he reconsidered that maybe she didn't have a bloodthirsty side. She'd certainly had chance enough to finish him off. Instead, she cleaned him up and was trying to help him get better.

However, if she hadn't killed his friends, who or what had? A sense of profound dread ran over him at the possibility of a killer at large. She said she was not the only one of her kind and that she brought him here to keep him safe. Was he still in danger of being killed?

Those short-lived moments of peace were now severely shattered.

He stayed there for a long time, gathering his strength to attempt getting back into the bed. Taking a deep, steadying breath, he pulled himself up, allowing himself to cry out in pain since he was alone. He collapsed in a puddle of sweat from the effort, winded.

All he wanted at this exact moment was to be home in his own bed, not on this lumpy mattress, and certainly not with a species that killed his, no matter how beautiful she was.

He lay there, going over that horrible night, again and again. He thought about everything that had happened up to this point and tried to think if she'd ever shown any aggression toward him. She hadn't.

No, she had never hurt him. He wasn't sure about what had actually happened, but a pang of guilt swept over him as he realized he might have been wrong, and he might have hurt her.

* * *

Serena returned hours later as daylight was fading and darkness was creeping into the cabin. She did not look at Jack or speak to him. She simply handed him a bag labeled "Burger King." She then turned away to put what looked like a *People* magazine on the counter. His eyebrows popped up. It was so incongruous to see her with that, something so human, so socially relevant. Yet, she had embraced it like it was a prized possession.

"Thank you," Jack uttered, but Serena made no response.

She stoked the fire, bringing the light up in the room, and set about lighting candles and kerosene lamps all around. It gave the room a hypnotic glow.

Serena lowered her weight into the chair and flipped through the magazine.

Is she actually sitting here reading People magazine?

Jack pulled himself up, slowly in an effort to minimize the pain. He peered up at Serena and caught her eyes as they flickered to him and then returned to the magazine. When he was fully sitting up, he breathed in deeply to calm his body and opened the bag. How strange it was that she had brought him a cheeseburger, from Burger King of all places. How had she gotten that? And the *People* magazine to boot?

Jack bit into the cheeseburger and groaned in appreciation. It was the best burger he had ever had. And it was gone in three bites. He had never been so happy to see a second one in the bag in all his life.

As Jack ate, he'd occasionally steal glances at her. But she remained stoic and focused on her reading material, like it held the secrets of the universe.

"Okay, look, I don't think you killed my friends," Jack conceded and dropped his hands on his legs, fries flying through the air. "I don't know what I thought, but I jumped to conclusions, and I'm sorry."

Serena regarded him but didn't reply. She simply twisted her hands together nervously.

Jack waited for what seemed like hours, and then finally spoke again. "Please say something."

"I did not kill your friends," she replied flatly, her eyes dark.

"I know. I just..." He sighed. "Look, I'm sorry. I've been locked up here in this cabin, going out of my mind worrying about what is happening at home, wondering what happened to my friends, and trying to fit all of this into some context that makes some sense to me, so cut me some slack."

Serena's lips quirked up into a grin. "All right. Slack will be cut." Her face returned to its grim line. "Next time, believe me. I will not lie to you. I may not be free to tell you everything, but I will not lie."

"Deal," Jack agreed as he tore off another bite of cheeseburger.

Looking around, he realized his fries were all over. "I made a mess." He reached out, trying to pick up as many as he could. Aside from everything weird going on, the cheeseburger and fries seemed to anchor him back to reality. Things like Burger King, Starbucks, and Pizza Hut did exist. He missed his job as a firefighter and his small house on the outskirts of Presque Isle. Right here and now was not his reality, just a temporary trip through the twilight zone.

He watched Serena as she read. She was beautiful, in her odd way. Her raven hair gleamed in the firelight, and the paleness of her skin was like alabaster. His mind led him in an odd direction, and he wondered if she was just like a human woman in all other physical attributes. The consideration had him choking on his food.

Serena rushed over and patted him on his back. "Eat slower."

He attempted to reassure her he was okay as he choked, but he was embarrassed at where his thoughts had been going. When he stopped coughing, all he could think about was how close she was and how her warmth was seeping into him. Before he knew what he was doing, he reached out and took her hand in his.

It was dainty and small but strong. She didn't move as he turned it over in his and studied the lines on her palm, letting his fingertips trace down them. When Jack finally glanced back up, she had an odd look of fear on her face, but she stood there, gazing at him with her beautiful eyes. He had the oddest sensation of wanting to kiss her, but he immediately pushed that thought away.

Serena was the first to break the contact as she slowly pulled her hand away and turned to get a glass of water.

When she handed it to him, he took it but wouldn't look up at her. Confusion took over at what he had been thinking about her.

Chapter 5: **Jack**

Chris and Adam stood side-by-side, gazing down at Jack with eerie, glowing eyes and pale faces. They stood in the cabin with torn clothing, matted with dirt and blood. Jack looked down at himself and realized he was tied to the bed. He yanked hard on the bindings, but he was unable to move. The more he pulled, the tighter the rope bit into his wrists and ankles.

"Did you know I was in love with Barbara Jean? I hoped to ask her to marry me someday," Chris said blankly and took a small step toward Jack.

Jack shook his head. "I didn't know, Chris. I'm sorry."

Adam crept forward. "I was almost out of my probation."

Jack tugged on his bindings as they moved closer. He noticed their skin was ashy. "I'm sorry, Adam. Please say you aren't dead."

Why couldn't he get free? Chris and Adam inched nearer to him.

"We are dead, and it is your fault," Chris accused.

"No! It's not my fault. It's not!" Jack pled.

Adam grabbed onto his arms, his fingernails digging into his skin.

"It was your fault. You wanted to camp deep in the woods when we were warned of the danger."

"No! I didn't mean for you to get hurt!" Jack yelled. Chris reached him and jabbed his hand into his wound, burying it deep into his body.

Jack screamed and jerked awake. His gaze searched around the room, eventually landing on Serena as she leaned over him.

"Easy," Serena cautioned. "*Shhh*, it's okay. It was just a bad dream."

"Chris? Adam?" he asked.

"They are not here. It was just a dream," she reassured him, patting his arm.

He jerked his arm away and inspected it. It wasn't bound, and Chris and Adam were nowhere to be seen. He let go and fell back onto the mattress.

"God," he declared, and tried to keep his heart from hammering. It beat so hard he figured she must be able to hear it.

"I promise you, you are safe. I will not let any harm come to you. You have my pledge."

Gazing into her eyes, he realized how sincere she was. He nodded and then looked down as she moved away. Admittedly, he felt oddly protected, but that wasn't what was killing him as he sat here. No, it was the guilt eating him up, chewing his insides up like acid. It was an emotion he knew all too well, one he typically kept at bay by working. Yet, here it was hitting him squarely across the face. He had caused the death of someone he loved... again.

* * *

"Would you like to try to sit outside, Jack?" Serena asked early one morning after she had taken a cup from his hands. She stood relaxed, her other hand on her hips. "The sun is warm and the animals are moving around. Do humans like to sit in the sunlight?" Her gold eyes were warm and open, and it caused Jack's breath to catch.

"Yeah, I love the sun. Are you strong enough to help me outside?"

Her lips twitched with the hint of a grin. "Of course I am. I carried you here, did I not?" She offered a full-on smile and he couldn't take his eyes off of it. Despite the fangs, she was gorgeous.

A thought occurred to him and he lifted the blanket. "I only have on boxers." His cheeks warmed and he chuckled nervously.

She frowned slightly. "Do you mean your shorts? Do you need more covering? If so, you can wrap the blanket around yourself. But, I fear you might trip over it as you walk. It would ease me if you didn't use it. However, if you are uneasy with how you are dressed, I will try not to look at you." She stepped back and averted her eyes as if she were giving him some room.

Jack peeked under the covers at his boxers. There were like shorts, so maybe it wouldn't be such a big deal. He opened his mouth to say something when she interrupted him.

"I'm sorry if I am not supposed to gaze at you. I will confess I have already seen your shorts when I dressed your wound. I hope you forgive me for that," she whispered, glancing down at the floor with pain etched on her face.

"No, it's okay," he said, hands raised. "I just didn't want to embarrass you. I'm okay with it if you are."

She lifted her eyes to meet his and the tension seemed to melt away as she grinned. "I am okay. Come. Let's go into the sunlight." She extended her hand, and he didn't move for a moment as he stared at her beckoning to him. God, she was so gorgeous, so utterly beautiful. He fought the urge to pull her to himself. He chased the thought from his head.

Bracing his side, he swung his legs over and the soles of his feet rested on the rough wood floor. She was next to him in a moment, her arms gently wrapping around him.

He breathed her in, and his heartbeat pounded in his ears at her closeness. He shook his head in an attempt to not think about her hands on his body, and how her warmth seemed to seep into his thirsty soul.

It was no effort for her to lead him out. Try as he might not to lean on her, he knew he couldn't help some of it, and she accepted his weight with little more than a small breath. Good lord, she was strong.

Breaking through the door, Jack inhaled the scent coming off of a small patch of wildflowers in a nearby field. The sun was just starting its trek across the sky, and it sat so low the light only reached his feet. Serena guided him to the small porch stairs. She maneuvered him to the first step. As he sat, he closed his eyes against the warm light kissing his face.

Serena disappeared and returned with the blanket and held it out to him. "For you, if you still feel you need it."

Jack smiled at her consideration. "Thanks." He laid the blanket across his midsection, but left his legs exposed to the bathing light. The warmth wrapped around him and he sucked in a deep breath. "God, this is great. Thank you."

"You're welcome," she replied and sat down on the same stair as him but kept her body as close to the edge on the other side. Inches separated them, but he could sense the unspoken distance she was trying to create.

She let out a sigh and raised her face. Her eyes were closed and she smiled. "The forest is happy today," she breathed out on a shudder.

He eyed her as he grinned. "Happy? Happy how?"

Serena's eyes opened and they seemed to almost twinkle. "The animals, they are at peace. For them, this is happiness."

"*Huh*," he declared and rubbed his chin. "And you know they are at peace how? Because they are quiet?"

She angled her body toward him, her expression alight with awe. "My kind can feel them. We can hear them like another animal would."

A pleasurable shock rolled through him. "Like you can hear

me? What do they say?" Jack pushed curiously.

She gave a short snort. "No, they do not talk exactly like you. They radiate an emotion, and we—the Shilund—can understand it. When they are afraid, their energy is afraid and they give off a scent of fear." She leaned over and quickly inhaled and smiled. "Much like you are giving off—" She stopped and her jaw slapped shut.

His eyebrows rose. "Like what?"

She shook her head and focused on the field. "Today, the energy from the forest is contentment. No hunters are seeking out others as food, and they are free to forage the woods without fear of death. Some are even curious, about you."

Jack wasn't sure what possessed him to ask the next question, but it tumbled out of his mouth. "Are *you* curious about me?" It became important for him to know.

Her gold eyes emitted a heat that had his heart thudding. She bit her bottom lip, her fangs slightly showing.

"I will let you sit and enjoy the warmth. I will be back."

And just like that, she slipped off of the stairs and onto the worn path below. Her dark hair flowed behind her on the wind as she rushed into the forest and away from him. As she left, he saw a large gray animal start to follow her, but the flash was gone as quickly as it had appeared.

The desire to run after her had his muscles twitching in response. But he couldn't go after her. He gazed down to his hand and traced the lines there.

She hadn't answered him, but that wasn't the disturbing part. He wanted her to say she was as curious about him as he was of her. To admit she couldn't get him out of her mind any more than he could get her out of his.

* * *

With each passing day, Jack's strength returned, making him a little less vulnerable. He took short walks around the small cabin and even braved the agonizing steps out to the porch to sit with Serena during the day when she wouldn't come inside.

In the evenings, he'd fall asleep with her sitting in the chair by the far wall reading and would awaken to sunshine and light but she'd be gone. Eventually, she would show up with food from different fast food places and new reading material.

The distance between them loomed, as if she was already trying to say goodbye to him. Even though they talked more, Serena began to shut him down emotionally, avoiding the simplest of personal questions. He just couldn't get around her walls. Their conversations always turned to him—how old he was, where he lived, did he have family, and what his life was like. She seemed to want to know everything about him. A small part of him was pleased that she was so interested, but it annoyed him to no end that she was truly closed off about herself. All he really knew was that she was a Shilund and lived alone in the tiny cabin.

Maybe it was just as well, he would be gone soon and she would...what? Remain here, hidden in these dense woods, just as she had been before? That seemed wrong on so many levels. What kind of life could that possibly be? But looking as she did, he knew she would stick out like a sore thumb in his world, unless, of course, she had her teeth filed down and wore contacts.

He wished she had more of a life. He knew she longed for it in how she read the magazines and books every day for hours on end. If only he knew how to pay her back for nursing him all these weeks.

The monotony was irrevocably broken one morning in a violent way. Jack woke up to the birds chirping gaily in the trees outside and easily sat up. Pulling in a deep breath, he gazed around and discovered Serena was gone. He swung his legs over the side of the bed and stood. Everything in him responded, as it should. He had very little pain as he twisted from side to side. He smiled. Relief washed over him as he took inventory of his body, letting his finger run over the new scar forming on his side. It was tender but dull. Dull was good. Except for the occasional mild, pulling pain in his side, he felt well enough to go outside and take a walk alone. But he wanted to be dressed.

Searching around the cabin, he found his clothes, laundered and neatly folded on the shelf, though they still had faint bloodstains on them. Next to his clothes were his shoes and socks. It was probably a good idea to get dressed and start figuring out how to get home. God, he hated the thought of leaving Serena and that really surprised him. In the midst of his healing, he had actually come to care about her. And wasn't that just crazy?

Walking around the room, he took in how bare it truly was. Her personal effects consisted of a plate, a cup, some silverware, and a couple of books. Nothing else. No pictures. No clothing. Nothing. And come to think of it, she only ever wore the same black sweater and pants. Although, she never smelled bad. Always the scent of sweet, fresh pine.

He gazed out the window at the sun filtering through the trees in sharp rays; their golden light broke the shadows apart like buttery pillars. As he studied the dust dancing, a feral face appeared before him, eyeing him with a curled lip.

Jack recoiled so quickly that he landed with a thud on his backside. With deft speed, the creature was inside the cabin and on top of Jack, beating him in the face. Jack responded by swinging his fists and striking it hard in the head. That succeeded in momentarily stunning it. Their eyes met in a terrifying moment. His eyes were exactly like Serena's, only his irises were a chocolate brown.

He was a Shilund, like Serena, but decidedly male. His canines were bigger, and his body was muscled and stern beneath a green army jacket and leather pants. His light brown hair was long and pulled into a ponytail. The Shilund growled and pulled back to strike again, when suddenly, his weight was lifted off Jack. It was a blur of movement as the man was thrown across the room. A fierce snarl echoed off the walls.

Jack was confused to find Serena standing in front of him in a protective stance, baring her fangs to the man lying across the room. She was impressive...and scary. Jack stood up, only to be held back by Serena.

"Don't move!" she ordered Jack.

The man was up in a moment, his chest heaving with anger. He was like a wild animal, with his snarling grimace and strands of long hair having escaped the tie that held the rest. His fists were clenched.

"What is this?" the Shilund man demanded through gritted teeth as he pointed to Jack. "You have a human here!"

"This does not concern you, Rahfey!" Serena spat, holding her stance before Jack.

"I can—" Jack began.

"No!" Serena cut him off.

Jack wanted to protest, but he clamped his mouth shut.

"Doesn't concern me? Are you crazy, Serena?" Rahfey began to pace. "You have this human here with you. You are breaking the law!"

"No one needs to know this," Serena argued. "You can turn and leave exactly as you came." She indicated the door with an incline of her head.

The room quieted, leaving only the heavy panting of Serena and Rahfey. Jack's heartbeat thrummed in his ears.

Rahfey took a step forward, and Jack attempted to get in front of Serena to pull her behind him. Whatever was going to happen, he didn't want her hurt. Not for anything.

Serena pushed Jack back. "Stop! He won't hurt me!"

Jack tried not to be moved, but Serena easily pushed him behind her. Man, she was strong.

Rahfey inched another step forward. "Baden will rain down hell on this place knowing a human is here...alive. You know the law. This will not pass."

"Baden doesn't need to know." Serena walked closer to Rahfey. "You can keep this to yourself. The human is only here long enough to heal and leave."

Rahfey quivered with rage, as his eyes trailed over Jack. "He looks well enough now. Are you sure it was only to let him heal?"

Serena seemed taken aback. "Of course. Why else would I allow a human here?"

"I don't know, Serena. You tell me." His fierce eyes glowed with suspicion as he bared his teeth to Jack.

Cue the *Jeopardy* music. Neither party moved, but stared at each other poised for battle.

Rahfey shifted slightly, his hand moving toward the inside of his robe, slowly revealing a gleaming blade.

Her movement was so fast that Jack could not track it. One moment, Serena was with him, and the next, she had Rahfey against the wall, holding him up by his throat, his legs dangling in midair. The blade dropped harmlessly to the ground.

The noise coming from her was animalistic and low. "You. Will. Not. Touch. Him." The menace was clear. Serena pushed Rahfey farther up the wall, waiting for him to respond. He could only manage to scratch at her hand to loosen it, but he was unsuccessful.

Rahfey struggled, his voice a whisper. "...let...me...go."

Serena continued to growl as she held him, squeezing tighter, which only succeeded in turning Rahfey's face into a mask of panic as all air was completely cut off. He began to lose consciousness.

"Serena!" Jack shouted, hoping to catch her attention. He didn't want her to kill him, even though he couldn't care less for Rahfey. Causing the death of someone else was a pain no one should ever live with.

Serena's eyes flickered toward Jack in acknowledgment of her name, and she released Rahfey. He landed in a tangled mess.

Rahfey coughed and struggled for breath, pulling in air as

deeply as he could. Grasping his throat, he glared up at Serena.

Serena squatted down in front of him and spoke between clenched teeth. "Get out of my house. And if you breathe a word of this to anyone, I will gut you. Do you understand?"

Rahfey stared at her, still attempting to breathe. He made no effort to answer her.

Serena grabbed the blade from the floor and held it to his throat. Rahfey froze.

"I asked if you understood?" She scowled at him unflinchingly.

"Yes," he answered begrudgingly.

"Good," she replied as she stood and dropped the blade at his feet. "Now, get out."

Rahfey gathered himself, weaving like a drunk, and paused at the front door, turning his fierce eyes on her. "One day, Serena, you will regret this. Mark my words."

Her only response was to snarl at him again as she stepped in front of Jack, her arm on him protectively. Rahfey reluctantly turned and disappeared into the golden sunlight streaming in through the door.

Jack relaxed, and sat back on the bed rubbing his head. What just happened here? Who was this Rahfey character, and why did he act like someone had pissed in his Wheaties?

Serena wheeled around to him. "What are you doing out of bed?" she demanded, her arms crossing defiantly.

The abrupt change in subject caught him off guard, and he threw his palms up to her. "*Whoa, whoa, whoa.* Wait one minute. Who was that?"

Serena's face flickered before resuming its glower. "He is...a friend."

"A friend? You've got to be freaking kidding me. If that's a friend, I'd hate to see an enemy. Why was he so mad? And who is Baden?"

Serena averted her eyes and made to turn away, but he grabbed her arm to prevent the motion and leveled his gaze on her. "Are you going to tell me or do I need to go running and ask Mr. Leather Pants myself?"

Serena angrily jerked away and marched over to the window. "I'm...they..." Serena sighed heavily and waved her hands in surrender. As she paced, her tone was threaded with panic. "I told you, my kind kills your kind. It is against the law to interact at all." Her hand went to her forehead and massaged it. Conflict was written in her furrowed brow and tight lips.

Jack eyed her as he considered her words.

"Why do they kill us and why is it against the law for us to be around each other?" Jack paled. "It *was* one of your kind that killed my friends, wasn't it?" Jack blurted as he rushed toward her. Worry marred her every step. He reached out and stopped her, forcing her to meet his gaze. He raised his eyebrows in a question.

"Yes," Serena admitted with a soft growl.

Fire licked up his insides. He was no longer afraid, but furious. "Was it this Rahfey who killed them?"

Jack waited and her silence told him the answer. His legs propelled him toward the door. He was going to find Rahfey and tear him limb from limb, even though he'd probably be killed before he got the chance. This was all so wrong. So wrong.

Serena caught his arm.

Jack paused and looked angrily down at her hand. Jerking up his head, he was expecting resistance or fury. Instead, she looked dubious, almost pleading.

"What?" he yelled, louder than he'd intended. "Are you going to keep me here, against my will? I will not let your *friend*," he sneered, "get away with this. I might be human, and he a Shilund, but I won't let this go."

"You would not be able to catch him," she conceded. "Plus, it was not he who killed them."

"Oh yeah? Then take me to whoever it was, since you apparently know." He spun around to face her. She stepped back, just a small step, but it was a sign of some sort of resignation.

"I cannot and will not. If I take you to them, they will finish the job that someone started with you. They will also kill me. They will think me...tainted. It would condemn us both."

Jack turned away, his jaw clenched and his fists closed. He didn't want her to die, and no matter what he thought of her kind, she had saved him. Plus, he did have some feelings for her, though he'd never admit that to her. Hell, he didn't even like admitting it to himself.

Stockholm syndrome, here I come.

He knew he should just let this go and focus on what he needed to do. He needed to go home. Sucking in a deep breath, he began. "You need to take me out of this forest and allow me to get back home." He turned to study her.

She looked pale, even for her. Her brow furrowed, and she was silent for what seemed like ages.

"Okay." Her voice was soft and melodic, much like when he'd first woken up in the cabin. "I will take you tonight." She averted her gaze and rushed out the door.

For some unknown reason, he wanted to stop her, to chase after Serena and pull her into his arms. Instead, he allowed her to leave and had to keep telling himself this was for the best. After all, he needed to get home, to see Chris and Adam's families, and try to figure out how to explain what had happened to them. He shouldn't want to stay here, should he? How stupid was that? But he wanted to nonetheless, and it made him question if he knew himself at all.

* * *

Following behind Serena in the woods at nightfall, Jack's skin crawled like they were being watched. The fact he couldn't see through the darkness only succeeded in making the hair on the back of his neck stand on end. Serena assured him it was safer to travel without illumination, but it was spooky. Her shadowy figure moved fluidly and barely registered a sound. Had she not been so close, he would have been lost.

The forest was so dense and thick it was like standing in the midst of hundreds of invisible people, all watching and not saying a thing. It was so overwhelming that he was sure someone would reach out and grab him at any moment. He was exposed and wished for a knife, a gun, or anything to protect himself. But he was at the mercy of this black forest and the beautiful Shilund leading him.

They walked for most of the night, his side protesting throughout the journey, but he ignored it. He was anxious to get out of the woods. As the sky was beginning to lighten, they broke through the forest into a parking lot. There sat a lone car, and Serena approached it without hesitation.

The door cracked open, and a girl, no older than nineteen, stepped out, illuminated by the car dome light. She was short, maybe five-foot-one, with red hair pulled into a ponytail. She had a cute face, slightly round and freckled.

"About time you got here, Serena. I've been here all night, and I've been very creeped out. I don't know what is in these woods...well, besides your kind," the girl huffed.

"I'm sorry, Vivienne. We walked as quickly as we could." Serena smiled apologetically. "Jack Day, this is Vivienne Jamison. She will take you back to town."

Vivienne grinned and reached out her hand to Jack while looking him up and down. "Viv, just call me Viv, everyone does. And let me say, I totally understand why Serena saved you."

Serena growled at Vivienne in warning.

"What?" Vivienne protested, feigning offense as she dropped her hand before Jack could actually shake it. "You know he's cute. Come on, even you have to see that."

"I'm right here." Jack pointed to his chest, feeling the need to alert Vivienne to his presence.

Vivienne shrugged.

"I don't have to see anything." Serena roughly pushed Jack toward the small car. "You must get in and go. You can trust Vivienne; she is a friend."

Now that was interesting. Serena had a human friend, and one he remembered seeing around town. He wasn't expecting that. But that explained all the Burger King and magazines. She must be her connection to the human world.

Vivienne leaned against the open car door and waited.

"Serena?" Jack pulled Serena a few steps away and gazed down at her. The darkness frustrated him; he couldn't see as clearly as he would have liked in the faint light of daybreak. "I can't begin to thank you for saving me. You didn't have to, but I'm glad you did." He wanted to throw his arms around her but thought she might not like it.

Oh, why not? He pulled her to him slowly. Surprisingly, she let her body fall into his, and he thought how well she fit there. His body rejoiced in it.

He wrapped his arms around her, allowing his hands to softly caress her back. "I hope I see you again. I don't know how, but I'd really like to. Maybe someday..." His voice trailed off.

She finally reciprocated, and for a brief moment, she hugged him back. He closed his eyes and let himself absorb her warmth, when, suddenly, she pulled away. He stared after her as she disappeared into the darkness in a blur. Before she left, Jack could have sworn he heard her whisper "Someday."

* * *

Jack stared out the windshield at the car's white beams of light cutting through the blue-black of the fading darkness as they sped out of the forest. It was odd sitting in a car again. Like, everything was normal, yet he was climbing out of the rabbit hole and back into the real world.

As they made their way toward town, Jack didn't want to talk. All he could think about was Serena. His heart ached. He hoped she would be okay. He didn't want to be the cause of her having any trouble. He truly hoped that Rahfey character would keep her secret.

"...and you know she is like the coolest person...*er*...yeah, that I have ever met."

Vivienne had been talking non-stop since they left the parking lot. Jack was relieved that she had. Her incessant chatter actually distracted him from the disappointment gripping him along with the gaping hole growing in his chest. Absently, he rubbed his torso, hoping he could massage the tightness away.

"So?" Vivienne asked.

Jack's head turned to her. "What? I'm sorry? What did you ask?"

"I asked, where would you like to be dropped? I'm guessing the police station since you have been missing for two weeks. They found your friends about a week ago, but they've still been going into the forest to search for you."

"They found Chris and Adam?"

"Yes." Vivienne spoke matter-of-factly, and then for the first time since they had been driving, she was quiet.

Jack shifted. "Do they know what happened to them?"

Vivienne's hands tightened on the wheel, her lips pursed. "A wild animal attacked them. They think it was a cougar, and that you are probably dead, too. There will probably be a lot of 'Thank you, Jesus' relief when you show up," she observed.

"Wild animal? They don't know about...?"

"The Shilund? No. You need to keep that secret. Do you understand?" Vivienne kept turning her head to see if he was making any type of affirmative acknowledgment. Finally, Jack nodded.

He understood all right. If anyone knew about her, they would probably kill her, and he'd never want that. The thought of anyone hurting her made him want to damage something or someone. He drew in a deep breath to clear his mind.

"She's the best friend I've ever had. And I wouldn't take it too kindly if you outed her and her kind," she charged.

Jack raised his hand in resignation. "I understand. I don't want her outed any more than you do. I promise." He paused for a moment. "So, it was you that gave her all the food for me?"

She smiled. "Yep. Serena wasn't sure you'd like anything she'd eat, I guess. She wouldn't tell me much about you other than you were human. I made the connection after they found Chris and Adam."

"How did you come to meet her?"

Her lips turned up in a smile and she glanced over to him.

"Just like you, she saved my life. Kind of a habit of hers, apparently." Vivienne chuckled.

"Apparently," he agreed. "So what happened?"

Vivienne waved her hand around dismissively. "Car wrecked into a river. A few more seconds and I would have been dead."

Jack nodded. Just like him. A few more seconds and he would have been dead.

Vivienne nodded as she turned onto the main street in town. "So, fair warning, if you reveal anything about her to anyone, I'll come after you. Just know, though I be but little, I am fierce. I know how to avenge my friends," she warned.

"Sure thing, William Shakespeare," he whispered, gazing out the window to watch the sleepy town streak by. "Like I promised, I'm keeping her a secret. I'm not sure what to say to everyone about what happened, but I'll figure something out that doesn't include her or her kind."

This seemed to appease Vivienne and she let out a deep breath. "Okay, where do you want to be dropped off?" Her thumb nervously drummed the wheel of the car as she slowed.

He thought for a moment. "The police station is good."

He considered what he was going to tell them. How could he explain being gone for two weeks? God, this was going to be a mess. He hoped Henry was on duty. It would either make things easier, or exponentially harder.

A few minutes later, they pulled up to the side of a pale brick building with the giant, neon *Police* sign.

Vivienne put the car in park and turned to Jack. He hesitated, considering he had to exit the car to go inside. Part of him didn't want to. Getting out of this car meant he'd be saying goodbye to his last connection to Serena. He didn't want to just leave.

"Do you have paper and a pen?" he asked.

Confusion flitted across her face. "Yeah. Why?" She reached into the back seat area and retrieved an *Ulta* catalog, tearing off a blank piece. Then scavenged around in between the seats until she found a pen.

He wrote down everything he could think to leave with her and handed it back.

Vivienne glanced down at the paper. "What is this?"

"If she needs me that is where she or you can contact me. Okay? I know she can't call me, but you can. If she needs anything, I don't care what it is. Okay?" He knew she might not ever use this or contact him, but it was worth a shot. At least Vivienne would know.

"Okay," she agreed slowly, studying the paper once more.

Jack opened the door, and as the inside of the car lit up, he noticed her reading his name, phone number, and address printed in neat block writing on the page. He leaned down to look at Vivienne once more.

She tapped the paper and nodded. He started to shut her door but she stopped him.

"Hey, you hang out with that deputy guy, right? That tall drink of water named Henry Parrish?"

"Yeah?"

"*Umm*, is he single?" Her blue eyes danced in the glow of the dome light.

"Really? You're asking about Henry?"

"Yeah," she replied like it was so obvious. "And in case it slipped your notice, I tend to keep very much to myself. I mean, I know who you are, but I don't *know* you. I'd sure love to know him."

Jack gaped at her and shook his head.

"Incredible," he muttered.

"So? Throw this very single lady a bone."

When he gazed at her again, he could see that though she was making light of this, she truly wanted to know about Henry.

"Yeah, he's single."

"Excellent! Can you—"

"No," he said, cutting her off. "Thanks for the ride." He shut the door before she could reply.

He didn't move as she put the car in gear and pulled off, bathing him in the red glow of taillights. Once she was far enough away, he took in a deep breath and turned to walk into the station.

Chapter 6: Serena

Serena watched Jack linger by the car as she hid in the shadow of the trees. He glanced around, almost as if he were searching for something. Was he searching for her? She hoped so. She bit her lip to keep from crying. It was a weakness and not something she wanted to allow herself. Still, no matter how she tried, the tears wanted to come.

A sharp ache pierced her chest as Jack got in the car with Vivienne and it pulled away.

Instinctively, she ran and followed the car as it made its way out of the woodland. The speed of the car was no match for a Shilund's running, so she was able to easily keep up. But the farther away it moved, the more pain she suffered. It was an involuntary need to be as close to Jack as long as she could. She wanted to make sure Vivienne and Jack made it out safely and that no Shilund attempted to stop them.

When no one did, she breathed a sigh of relief. Rahfey had kept her secret. He was more honorable than she'd ever suspected, and a pang of regret gripped her at having treated him so harshly. But she had to protect Jack, at all costs.

As the car made it to the where the woods thinned out, and the pavement cut through the sparse fields, Serena stopped and watched the car disappear, all the while feeling like her heart was going with the two humans.

Letting her body rest against the rough bark of a tree, she panted as if in extreme pain and slid down to plant herself in the soft moss. Tears streamed down her face and her breath hitched.

Woodland animals moved closer to her, their life force sending a sympathetic assurance at the agony she radiated. But nothing could reassure her. She had lost the one thing that had ever woken her up from this veiled existence. But his life was in the human world, and hers was here in the woods.

The sharp pain shooting through her body was overwhelming. She wondered if she had somehow hurt herself running behind the car in the woods. But no, she didn't think she had. This foreign pain radiated from deep inside. Her grief was all about Jack leaving.

She missed him.

Laying her head on her knees, she closed in on herself and

sobbed. That was when she heard the crackling of small twigs under the weight of something large. She knew who it was. Alaric. She sensed his questions before she saw him. As she glanced up, dark eyes inched closer. The gray wolf sniffed around her for a moment, looking for the cause of her injury. When he saw none, he slowly turned and found a comfortable spot to lie down on, right beside her leg, his head held high as if guarding her. Her keening must have drawn him to her.

Alaric's badly scarred paw was stark against the darkness of the ground. She remembered their meeting last summer, when he had been caught in a trap and was on the verge of gnawing it off to get away. She reassured him she meant no harm and freed him from the trap. After that, he and his pack roamed close to the Siege, and to her whenever she was in the woods.

Serena reached out and brushed his coarse fur with her hands as she cried, his emotions seeping into her in an attempt to comfort. But, she was barren in this moment and nothing could comfort her. So, she let herself weep.

* * *

The sun was blazing brightly overhead by the time Serena made her way back to the cabin. Alaric had followed her the entire trip, watching her to make sure all was well. She stopped at the bottom of the steps and keened, telling him she was okay.

He turned and disappeared into the heavy brush.

As she stood at the door, she realized she didn't want to go inside. Going inside meant knowing Jack was gone and she was alone again.

She had never minded being alone all these months. What her clan had meant as a punishment had been her saving grace. Being alone had only solidified her resolve to continue as she had. She wasn't going to bend to their expectations, no matter what they did.

But now, being alone meant being without Jack and that was a punishment. The pain in the realization was overwhelming, and she stood with her hand hovering over the doorknob. She needed to just turn the handle and go in. Like ripping off a bandage, she needed to do it quickly, so she forced herself inside.

The cabin was just as she had left it. The fire was banked and the bed was made. The air was stale from the lack of movement.

She sighed. She wanted to see Jack here, moving around, telling her about his human life. Missing him was like a monster in the room. The lack of his presence was a thing unto itself.

Sitting in the chair, she fingered the black cloak that hung over it. She recalled the last time she'd worn it, when she'd rescued Jack from the attack. That night, as she sat on her porch, staring up into the starry sky, the animals' distressed chatter over the violence had caught her attention and driven her to find out what was happening.

She'd raced as quickly as she could and was shocked to scent Shilunds that were familiar to her, from her very clan. She didn't have time to say anything, just grabbed the only human she could and pulled him to safety.

The entire way back to the cabin with Jack, she tried to reason why they had attacked the humans. Granted, growing up in the Siege, she had heard about Shilunds killing for sport, but she had never witnessed it. Was that what had happened? She couldn't understand the animosity toward humans.

Seeing the helpless humans being dispatched had forced her to act. She was glad she had. She pictured Jack's smiling face in her mind and realized it had all been worth it. He was safe and home. He would continue his life as if the attack had never happened. She only wished she could act like she hadn't met him, but she couldn't. He had left an indelible mark on her.

She climbed into the bed and wrapped herself up in the covers that still bore his scent.

"I miss you, Jack," she whispered into the night, letting herself be swallowed by the grief. In the distance, Alaric bayed.

Chapter 7: Jack

Jack hated talking to his mom while she wept on the other end of the phone. She asked him repeatedly if he really was all right.

He paced around the living room of his small house, his wrist still bearing the tag the hospital had made him wear. His ear was hot from the phone, and he paced around in his living room to keep from losing his mind. Finally, the space was not large enough, and he walked from room to room in his house while they talked.

Her crying took him back to Lilly and the way she'd sobbed for months after her death. It was all his fault, he reminded himself. His. No one else's. He didn't want his mind to go there, and he found himself turning over the family photo that included Lilly as he stalked around his bedroom.

"Please don't cry, Mom," he begged. He was going to have to find a reason to hang up if she didn't stop. He was going to lose it, he really was.

"Oh, Jack," was all she could get out between the sobs.

He kept reassuring her that he was fine. That he had been to the hospital, checked over, and talked to the police at length. Then his mother would calm, only to start crying again. He couldn't take it. Relief washed over him when his dad got on the phone.

He collapsed onto the edge of his bed, holding his head in his hand. He inhaled deep breaths to calm himself down.

"Jack? Son, I'm so glad you're okay." His deep voice cracked.

"Yeah, I'm fine. Dad, I'm sorry that you guys thought I was dead. But I'm okay, I promise. Can you try to get Mom to calm down?"

"I'll try, but your mom has been a wreck for two solid weeks. She just wouldn't believe you were dead. She called the park ranger's station and the police every day. She got really ramped up when they found the bodies of Chris and Adam. I'm truly sorry about them being killed. Their parents must be inconsolable right now..."

Jack's chest tightened; his two best friends were gone, ripped apart by the Shilund, and he could never tell anyone what really happened.

His father continued, "You know, they have been looking for that cougar, but they haven't found it yet. I hope they do soon, so this doesn't happen again. I'm just glad you got away."

"Yeah, me too," Jack whispered. "Hey, Dad? I'm really tired, and I haven't bathed since I've been gone. I'd like to get a shower and go to bed."

"Oh, of course. Well, we love you and we're so glad you're okay. Call us later, all right?"

"Sure, Dad. Love you, too." Jack slowly pressed the button on his phone, hanging up the call. He let his head hang heavy between his shoulders, thinking about all the grief he had caused them over the course of his life.

Lying back on his bed, he stared at the ceiling and couldn't stop his thoughts from wandering to Serena. It blew his mind that anything like her even existed. He wondered how many were out there and why they'd attacked them? The only thing they were guilty of was hiking far into the woods to primitive camp, nothing more. They didn't do anything unsavory or questionable. So, why attack once it got dark?

He strained hard to remember what had happened. But again, he only could see the flash of green, and then it was lights out for him. It was like his mind was keeping him from seeing that night clearly. Maybe it was a Godsend. The image of Chris with a spear sticking out of his chest was horrifying. When he tried to think harder to recall all the details, he would get a show-stopping headache. It was infuriating not being able to remember it clearly.

He decided that a good, long shower was what he needed. Once under the spray, he let his head drop, the warm water relaxing his muscles and washing away the grime. He braced his hands on the tile wall and thought of Serena. Glancing down to the angry, red line of his healing wound, he thought if it weren't for her, he would have been killed like Adam and Chris.

Adam and Chris. He'd never see them again. The agony from that thought bubbled up in his chest and hit him like a sledgehammer. It was because of him—he had caused their deaths. Old guilt gripped his heart like a vise and squeezed hard.

He dropped down in the shower, unable to support his weight under the grief. Sitting back against the wall, he began to cry at the loss of them. He cried because he wanted to tell them he was sorry he had let them down and that he'd miss them every moment of his life. How could he ever make up for this? He'd been trying to make up for the time before his entire life, but it never seemed to make a difference. No, he was a destroyer and no amount of penance and praying were going to make it any better.

Chapter 8: **Serena**

Three days had passed, but it seemed like three years to Serena. She hadn't wanted to eat or do anything but sleep. Eventually, she knew she needed to get up and at least see Vivienne.

How things had changed for her in such a short amount of time. Only three months ago, she had been staying in the Siege, largely an outcast, but happily living with Arn. She'd learned to read human books and understand things like mathematics and even some human culture, though it had been limited to what Arn could tell her. Arn had lived among the humans at one point in his life but kept the particulars secret even from her. Still, he had shared some details with her. It made her less frightened of the human world and increasingly curious about it.

Serena approached the window and peered out. She remembered how she was brought out here as a punishment by the clan, to break her with the loneliness this cabin brought. The idea was that she'd eventually want to fall in line with what was expected of her in the Siege. Instead, it only made her more determined to not be like everyone there.

She glanced at her hands. They were like a human's, the same long fingers and fingernails. She was flesh and blood exactly like them and if there were these types of similarities that were so easy to find, couldn't there be others? Why did Shilunds and humans have to be enemies? Certainly they had more in common than not.

She sighed heavily and leaned her head against the window. The cabin was feeling too small, and she had get out and away before she let herself buckle to the sorrow that was coursing through her like blood.

She hid in the wooded area outside of the Dairy Queen. Her eyes scanned for any type of danger, but there was none apparent, and no scent of any of Shilunds around. It was only adults guiding their wide-eyed children up to the slotted glass to order the various goodies and sugary treats from the girls inside. It somewhat fascinated Serena as the children giggled and squealed. Ice cream was pretty good. Vivienne had brought her some one time. She believed Vivienne had called it chocolate.

The small, white building stood out in contrast to its sparse surroundings. No other business was close by, which left more room for the barrage of patrons' vehicles in the large parking lot that spread out across its front. Around the building, the huddled masses were like refugees in their search of the much-needed oral satisfaction on the sultry September evening. It was summer's last gasp before fall took hold, and everyone was taking advantage.

Vivienne exited the back of the Dairy Queen, removing her apron, and summarily tossing it on the bench outside of the door. She searched around to see if anyone took notice of her, but no one had, so she started her circuitous route toward the wooded area.

They had been doing this for months now, Vivienne helping her learn about the world and things like pizzas, cell phones, books, and Brad Pitt. She was her doorway to this world and having her help made things easier. Serena had been raised to fear humans and the world outside of their Siege, but Vivienne changed her view completely.

Vivienne waltzed slowly into the density of the forest line, far enough back to see the Dairy Queen and yet be hidden.

"I'm here, Viv," Serena whispered, stepping out from her hiding spot.

Vivienne turned toward Serena, her face etched with frustration, and exhaled in a large burst. "It's about time. I've walked out here a couple of times to see if you were here. Where have you been? It's been three days since you dropped off Mr. Adonis with me. I've been worried sick. What gives?"

"I believe his name is Jackson Day," Serena corrected quietly.

Vivienne rolled her eyes. "You are so uneducated."

Serena's eyebrows pulled down. "You mean in human ways. I'm learning—"

"No, not just human ways," Vivienne interrupted. "Just being down with pop culture, in—you know what? Never mind. It loses its meaning when I have to explain it to you." Vivienne folded her arms and rested against a large elm, her expression melting from frustration to forced calmness.

"Well, I like when you explain things to me." Serena's voice was small, almost embarrassed. She found herself looking down at her hands. She hated feeling so stupid about humans and what Vivienne explained as "pop culture." Vivienne didn't know it, but the human world was where Serena wanted to be though she knew she would never belong. So, this small taste she experienced through Vivienne was enough for her if that was all she would ever be allowed.

"Me too, but I've got to do a better job. And it's okay, Serena. You'll get there. Anyway, where have you been? I was afraid your elders executed you, or tried to re-educate you."

Serena glanced at her nails and picked at them. "No, nothing like that. I just...well, I was sad. I didn't want to be around anyone."

"I've been worried. You haven't come to my house, and I checked for your ribbon a million times. Mine has been there for a few days." Vivienne pointed up to the large pine that served as the host of their signal, with its missing bark and broken, spike-like branch. They had devised a system of placing ribbons on the tree as a signal to meet. It wasn't a perfect system, but it worked.

"When you didn't let me know you'd be coming, I got really worried. As much as I hate the woods, I was ready to go searching for you. What took you so long to respond?"

Vivienne gave her a funny look and Serena quickly turned away, tears filling her eyes. Vivienne came close and patted her arm. "Oh, hon, are you missing Mr. Ad—*er*, Jack? Did you like him that much?"

Serena would not look up at Vivienne, and merely nodded her head. "I do like him. But I don't know why it feels like a hole has been punched through my chest. It's painful and I miss him."

A wide grin stretched across Vivienne's face. "Serena! Are you in love?"

"No. What? No. Leave it alone, Viv." Serena's face turned away in frustration.

That was a human thing she had read about in some of the magazines Vivienne had given her. Being in love was a desirable thing for human girls. But it sounded vulnerable and painful. She wasn't that, was she? She considered it very carefully, and then denied it to herself. All the while, a small part of her knew it was true.

Vivienne smirked while she watched Serena move around. "Okay." Vivienne reached into her pocket, pulled out a piece of paper, and smiled a devious smile. She tapped it on her hand and then gazed at Serena as she held it up. "You know, Jack gave me his phone number and address. I have it right here."

Serena's head jerked up, but she made no move toward Vivienne. Instead, she fixed her eyes on the little piece of paper her friend held. It was something he had touched. She wanted that paper for no other reason except it been in his hands.

Every part of her wanted to rush over, jerk it out of Vivienne's hand, and then figure out a way to call him. What would it be like to hear his voice again? She wanted it so badly that she could hardly speak. It was as if her life had stopped when he went away. Why was she feeling this irrational need to be near him?

Maybe this kind of feeling was why Shilunds rejected mating based on emotion. For the most part, there was blood binding that tied mates together for life, but emotion played no part in that. It was always for the greater good of the Siege and the proliferation of their race.

Serena sighed. "I cannot call him. I do not have a phone of any type, you know that."

Vivienne reached into her pocket with her other hand and pulled out a cell phone. She waved it, almost if she were waving a red curtain in front of a charging bull. "I got this for you. I figured it was the least I could do." Vivienne waited. "So, do you want the number and the phone?"

Serena wasn't sure she should take both, but everything in her wanted to. She wanted to be close to Jack and if it was only in hearing his voice, so be it. She surprised herself by going to Vivienne and taking both the phone and the paper. But really, she shouldn't be shocked by it; she was defying everything her clan stood for these days.

"Great! I knew you'd want it." Vivienne pointed to the phone. "I put my number in the phone already, so you can call me whenever you want. It will be easier than trying to make it every Tuesday and Thursday or tapping on my window in the dead of night, scaring the crap out of me."

Serena studied the phone, turning it over and over in her hand. She knew how to use it from playing with Vivienne's. All she had to do was dial this number and hit enter.

A scary thought filled her. "Do you think he'd like it if I called him?"

"*Duh*! Yes, of course. That's exactly why he gave me the number." Vivienne smiled. "You should call him tonight."

Serena nodded but stared down at the phone. Her heart thudded in her chest and her stomach clenched. She would be able to hear his voice through this device she held.

Serena wondered if he really did want to hear from her.

She thought of Jack. Was he close to being mated to a female? He hadn't mentioned any when he'd stayed with her. Then he was probably not intended for any female, and that gave her a giddy little feeling in her stomach. He must be free. She couldn't help but smile at her surmising.

Vivienne put her hands on her hips. "Oh, come on, Serena. Spill it."

Serena shook her head and smiled at Vivienne. She couldn't tell her that she couldn't allow herself to hope to be with Jack. He was human, she was Shilund. They could never be together, ever. Then there was the rule in her society that said the Overseers decided mating choices for females who didn't choose on their own by adulthood. She knew she was considered an adult, and if she didn't choose soon, they would choose for her. She shuddered at the thought of being thrown together with a male she didn't have this feeling for.

"What really happened out there in that cabin?" Vivienne prodded. "I've never seen you this enamored with anyone or anything before. You really do care for him, don't you?"

"Yes," she admitted in a whisper.

"Well, if he breaks your heart, I'm going after him. Just sayin'." Vivienne's face was stern.

"The heart is soft; it cannot break like a bone," Serena countered.

"Oh, it can break," Vivienne assured. "Into a million, splintered shards like a piece of glass."

Serena wanted to argue with Vivienne but decided she wouldn't. She'd try to figure out this latest colloquialism on her own. It was probably one of those sayings that tried to relate a strong feeling with an action. If a heart could break like a bone, she never wanted to experience it. How did one survive after that? She hoped she never found out.

"Thank you for the phone. That was kind of you." Serena moved to indicate the conversation should end so she could rush back to the cabin. She did not want to put Vivienne in any danger should another Shilund venture close to the road.

"Are you kidding? With as many times as you have bailed me out, never mind about rescuing me. Please! I owe you a lot. Plus, you are my best friend, and I love you. Oh, wait. Here, this is a battery pack for charging since you don't have electricity, but the plug is in there as well." Vivienne handed her a box. "Just keep the phone off unless you intend to use it. And call me too, not just Mr. Wonderful."

"Who?"

Vivienne pinched the bridge of her nose, shook her head, and started walking toward the edge of the woods. "I'll see you later, Serena! Love ya, chica."

Serena waved as she watched her friend walk determinedly away. She watched until Vivienne was out of the woods before turning to leave. Staring down at the phone, she wanted so badly to hear his voice. It was only a push of a button away.

A thrill rushed through her as she ran back to the cabin.

Chapter 9: Jack

Jack hated how out of touch he was with everything. He was in the firehouse, sweeping with a large, industrial broom, pushing out the dust and scattered leaves that had been tracked in. Try as he might, he couldn't get Serena, or the deaths of his friends, out of his mind.

Apparently, the firehouse had put on a great funeral for both of them, carrying their caskets to the graveyard on top of the tanker with flourish. Someone had videotaped it and he'd watched it in the break room, all the while chewing on his nails. The ceremony had honored them, and they truly deserved that. He really missed cutting up with them, his brothers-in-arms. He needed to know why this had happened. Serena hadn't told him much. What little she revealed did nothing to ease his mind; it only succeeded in causing more questions.

Leaning on the broom handle, he gazed out the open bay doors and watched as cars went by. It was a beautiful day, the sun shining and a breeze brushing through the building. But he couldn't allow himself to relax.

"Hey, Jack, how's the side feeling?" Bob Merchant, the fire chief, came up behind him, placing his hand on his shoulder. He was shorter, but stout and strong with a receding hairline. Bob was almost as old as Jack's father, but he was as healthy as any man half his age. Bob's dark eyes bore into his.

"*Eh*, it's healing slowly. Can't wait for it to completely heal so I can get back to going on calls with you guys. It's bad enough having me down, but with Chris and Adam..." Jack's voice trailed off.

"I know. It's such an awful shame about them." Bob brushed his hand through his thinning, chestnut hair and sighed.

Jack cleared his throat to keep from losing his composure. "So, is the chief from Ashland going to lend you some men?"

"Yeah," Bob spoke quickly, "two men are going to enter into our rotation starting tomorrow. I would have asked for three, but I think a shift can make do less one man. I'm going to stay on call just in case, as well."

"Well, that's good of them to do that."

Both men stared out of the doors, neither one wanting to say a word in the reverent silence.

Finally, Bob gently slapped Jack on the back and walked away.

Jack let out a deep breath and thought of Serena and where she was. She was the reason he was alive. Part of him felt a little guilty that she picked him, when it could have just as easily been Chris or Adam. They were, after all, better men than he was.

He knew some of this was probably survivor's guilt, but it didn't make him feel any less remorseful. Two good men were dead, men that had been his closest friends. He missed them terribly.

He could still hear their voices echoing around the firehouse: making snide remarks pointed playfully at Bob, giving Reynolds a hard time about his cooking, playing every kind of practical joke imaginable. Of course, Jack was an accomplice to all the antics. God, the loss of them hurt. He rubbed his chest, swallowed hard, and without realizing it, he glanced over to their lockers, which had been draped in black ribbons.

He couldn't fall apart here. He just couldn't. He tore his eyes away and began to sweep slowly, trying hard to focus on every little piece of debris beneath the bristles, anything to keep him from thinking about Chris...Adam...Lilly.

One day, he would find out what had happened to Chris and Adam, if it was the last thing he did.

Chapter 10: **Rahfey**

Rahfey stood on the top branch of a large tree near Serena's cabin. He watched as she raced into her place and shut the door. He searched around for any sign of the human male, but he could not see him anywhere, nor could he smell him on the air. It appeared as if Serena might have actually taken his advice and killed him.

Good, she needed to remember who and what she was.

Dropping thirty feet to the ground with little effort, he landed softly. Taking an appraising look around, he approached the cabin. Eyes stared back at him from the clearing's edge. It was that damned wolf that always follows her around. It gave a low growl and Rahfey growled right back. One day he'd kill that animal and wear his hide like a trophy.

He climbed the steps, knocked, and then stood back, leaning his weight against the post by the stairs. It took a moment, but Serena flung open the door.

"What do you want?" she spat. Her golden eyes seemed angry. Why did she have to be like that? She should be grateful he was here. He risked his very standing with the clan and the Overseers to be here in the midst of her shunning.

The stormy expression on her face didn't suit her.

"Do I need a reason to visit you? The Overseers will choose you as my mate. You know this, as do I. The sooner you accept what we are, the better." Let her argue against that.

Serena glared at him, fire burning in her eyes. "I am not yours, I will never be yours, and regardless of what the elders say, I will not be joined with you, ever. Shunning or not."

She turned and headed deeper into the cabin, leaving the door open. Rahfey took that as an invitation and entered. He was unaffected by her rejection. Some part of him believed she was simply playing hard to get.

"You know Arn would be happy to see us together. Besides, why would you want to be relegated to the rejected ones?"

"I do not know what Arn wants or doesn't want. He hasn't told me, and I haven't asked. I do know he'd want me happy, unlike the expectation of the clan to just comply regardless of feeling. So, please, Rahfey, just let this drop."

She leaned against the counter, looking uncomfortable. Maybe she realized he shouldn't be here as an unmated male, with an unmated female, even if she were to be his intended. Maybe she accepted tradition and rule more than he realized. That she appeared uneasy somehow pleased him.

Rahfey walked around the cabin, gazing around. "I see the human is gone, though I can still smell his stench."

"Yes, he is." Serena's tone was softer. "And thank you for not telling the council. I wasn't sure you were going to keep it to yourself."

"Why would I want my future mate killed?" He inched closer, wishing to touch her, and when she turned away from him it caused a fierce ache. He wanted to so badly. But he didn't want to scare her or push her too quickly. She'd be his someday. Of that, he was sure. He leaned in and inhaled her scent, letting it fill his lungs and settle his soul. She was warm and intoxicating, and he wanted nothing more than to have her in his arms and kiss her until she yielded to him. But he fought against it so as not to alarm her.

Finally, Rahfey smiled and made his way toward the door. "Well, I'll go now. I just wanted to see how you were, and I see you are fine and alone." He regarded Serena's face, which seemed forlorn. Maybe she was missing him. His heart thrilled at the thought.

Rahfey knew that this little blip on her rehabilitation would fade into obscurity. Soon, she'd be accepted into the fellowship of the Shilund again, and her penance would be over.

"Remember, I wasn't here. You keep my secret, and I'll keep yours."

She gave a small nod.

Grinning, he turned and walked out the door, pleased that it appeared life would soon go back to normal and he would get everything he wanted.

Chapter 11: **Serena**

Serena was relieved when Rahfey finally left and rushed after him to shut the door and bolt it. Hurrying to the window, she made sure he disappeared into the wood. She hadn't decided when she was going to call Jack, but her encounter with Rahfey certainly seemed to steel her resolve. She made her way to the counter and grabbed the phone. Keeping it hidden from Rahfey had been hard. She had worried he would discover it. She wasn't sure how he would've reacted if he had found it, but it wouldn't have been good.

She sat down with the phone in her lap, staring and tracing the face with her finger. Just a couple of punches of buttons were all she needed to do. Then he'd be there. Nothing was stopping her.

Her conscience waged war on her desires, and then duty decided to jump in on the argument and remind her who and what she was. She turned over the phone and considered the consequences of keeping contact with this human male. The Overseers would flay her. But, she admitted to herself, she didn't really care anymore what they did to her. In the end, she listened to her heart. She pressed the button down to power the phone on.

As soon as it did, a text message appeared from Vivienne.

Hey. Just wanted to see how you were. Did you call Jack yet?

Serena rolled her eyes. Vivienne could be so pushy. But Serena really loved her, like a sister, even though she made her crazy at times. Vivienne taught her so much about human life and was a good friend to her.

Serena pressed the buttons on the phone to respond.

I am fine, and no, not yet. Serena hit send and almost immediately, a reply came.

Rena! I'm glad to hear from you. What are you waiting for? Call him!

Vivienne, please do not keep asking me, okay?

Okay, I'll try, but promise me you'll tell me when you do.

I will, now goodbye.

Geez! Goodbye. Text me soon! I miss you.

Serena smiled. She missed her, too. But she needed to not go into town as much now, for fear the council would discover her crime of associating with the humans.

She stood up, paced around, then finally sat down again and

found the shortcut to Jack's phone number. Before she could change her mind, she hit send.

The phone took a moment to connect and then rang on the other end. Her heart threatened to beat right out of her chest. Finally, Jack's deep voice sounded through the earpiece.

"Hello?"

Her stomach did flip flops, and she couldn't quite find the words.

"*Uh*, hello? Anyone there?"

She cleared her throat. "Jackson Day? This is Serena."

"Serena?"

"Yes, you remember, from the woods?"

Jack laughed a deep, throaty laugh. "Of course I know who you are. I'm just surprised you have a phone. You said you didn't have one."

"Yes, well, I've only recently come into possession of one."

The line was quiet for a moment. "Well, I'm glad. It's so good to hear your voice. Are you okay?"

"Yes," she replied quickly. "I'm well. Are you healing okay?"

He sighed deeply. "Yes, but not as quickly as I'd like. But I went back to work this week, so at least I'm doing that."

"That's good."

The two were silent, their respective breathing the only noise.

"So, your people didn't give you any grief about me? I'd feel truly bad if they did."

"No, no one knows, except for Rahfey."

Jack chuckled. "He didn't seem inclined to want to keep a secret."

"No, I agree, but he didn't want to see me in more trouble, so he kept it quiet."

"More trouble?" Jack questioned.

Serena paused for a moment. "Yes, well, nothing to worry yourself with."

"Did I cause it?" His voice was sorrowful.

"No, you didn't."

"Good. That's good." Jack whispered, "Serena?"

"Yes?"

"Can I come and see you?"

Serena's heart leapt. He wanted to see her! She couldn't believe he actually wanted to see her. She most definitely wanted to see him.

"Do you want to?"

"Of course, why else would I ask?" Amusement was thick in his tone.

"I don't know. But I'm not sure it would be wise."

"Please, just a few minutes, somewhere safe for both of us."

"Jack...I..."

"Please," he begged, and she was hard-pressed not to give in.

Serena wanted to see him so badly it almost hurt. She knew her answer before she even spoke it. "Okay, can you meet me at the Dairy Queen out on Route 205 at six in the morning tomorrow? Dawn will be breaking, but it will still be dark enough to be safe. So wait in your car, and I'll be there. Park at the far end of the lot, near the wooded edge."

"Yeah, I can swing it. Oh and one more thing."

"Yes?"

"I'm really glad you called."

"Me too. Goodbye, Jack."

"Sweet dreams, Serena."

Then the phone went dead, the hollow sound in the receiver going dense. She smiled, thinking she'd see him in less than a day. She couldn't wait.

She stood up. Holding the phone to her chest, she twirled around the room.

Taking out the phone to text, she drafted a message to Vivienne.

Just talked to Jack. I will see him tomorrow.

Would she feel any different when she saw him again? Probably not. He was all she could think about every night and every day.

The phone dinged.

Nice! So is he coming to you or you to him?

I am meeting him where I do you, tomorrow morning.

No hookups in the parking lot now. It's not good to be caught in a car with your boyfriend. Happened to me once, bad news.

Hookups?

I forget you know so little. I'll explain later. TTYL.

Serena frowned. *TTYL?*

TALK TO YOU LATER!

Yes, you will.

Serena turned off the phone and hid it under her bed cushion. Lying back, she stared up at her ceiling and thought of Jack's blue eyes.

Chapter 12: Arn

The sleepy, gray light of morning was just beginning to invade the darkness when Arn walked out the entrance to the Siege, hidden in the hillside. The dense cover kept it fully obscured from the eyes of those who did not know it was there. The Shilund had hidden in this forest for hundreds of years. Other clans were scattered throughout Canada and the northwest United States, but his clan, the Sterling clan, had always been here.

Arn had wandered the lands when he was younger, meeting other Shilund leaders and seeing how they lived and ruled their areas. But he always returned to the safety of this territory, Sterling Territory, despite the hard-nosed way they lived, adhering to very old-world rules. He had simply missed home. So here he was, half obeying their rules, and doing just enough to keep his place.

The Sterling clan ruled this area and there had been no attempt at invasion in twenty years. This area was rich in natural resources and abundant in hiding places, so it was desirable to obtain. But the Sterling clan was always able to defend its territory and remain here.

The air was crisp, a forewarning to the encroaching autumn. Moving down the moss-covered hillside, he made his way to the babbling creek below. The water cut through the rich soil that resembled dark roasted coffee. He squatted down until he could put his hands in and rinse them off in the chilly liquid. Throwing some onto his neck, he liked how awake it made him.

His mind was on his daughter and how she was. He missed seeing Serena every day, but until her penance was up, he wasn't allowed to be around her or he risked punishment from the Overseers, more specifically, Baden.

The muscles in his shoulders tensed up as he thought of him. Ever since Arn returned to the Sterling clan, Baden had been a thorn in his side. Baden was, at every turn, watching Arn and waiting for a challenge to his leadership. But Arn never gave him reason to think he would challenge him. Arn was Anaximander, or the alpha Overseer, when he'd left, but his leaving forfeited the position. The only way to get it back was to challenge the current Anaximander, who just happened to be Baden. Arn didn't want it, and no matter how many times Arn reassured him, Baden was always tensed for a battle with him.

Rising, he sighed heavily and decided to walk some before he actually hunted. He wanted to stretch his legs and loosen his muscles. He started down a trail that circled the hill and was thankful for some time alone.

As he walked, his mind returned to Serena. He considered how much Serena looked like her mother and it made him smile, glad that some part of Sisika, or Sisi as she was nicknamed, lived on. Her mother had been lithe and beautiful, and he missed her deeply. With their long dark hair, those golden eyes, and the same face shape, they could have passed as sisters. But the physical resemblance stopped there. Sisi had not been as tall as Serena was now, and had been so much softer and quieter than Serena could ever imagine being.

Arn had always loved Sisi, even when she'd been mated to his best friend, Nathan.

When they died, he knew it was an honor and a responsibility to raise Serena on their behalves. But he didn't want Serena to ever feel like she had to be beholden to any man or any tradition, no matter what it was. He taught her to speak her mind and be more than she was expected to be by the clan. It was the one thing he could never give Sisi, but her daughter would be allowed to choose.

A dove flew over and landed in a tree branch, cooing softly to Arn.

"Sisika," he whispered and smiled. He decided he would stop by the cabin to check on Serena, but from a distance. He just wanted to see she was safe and getting along okay.

He took off running down the trail.

Chapter 13: **Serena**

The crisp September morning succeeded in putting Serena on high alert as she waited for Jack. She walked in darkness until she reached a tree with a good view, positioning herself high on a branch close to the lot to wait and watch to make sure no one had followed her.

But no one had. So, she anxiously awaited his arrival.

As she sat perched in the tree, she considered that her penance was almost over and how she'd be allowed back to the Siege. Funny, but the thought was not welcomed. Shilunds were largely pack driven, and everyone was expected to always act in the best interest of the clan. Individuality was spurned. But, she was different and always garnered the wrath of the Overseers. Her only reason for wanting to go back would be to see Arn. She missed him so much it hurt. Although she knew he was not her real father, he was the closest thing to one she had and the only family she had left.

Arn always supported her individuality in secret, but he warned her to keep that side hidden within the Siege. It was a tenuous situation within their walls when someone didn't comply. So, she walked a fine line between appearing to comply and being who she was. She did try to keep her desires secret, but time after time, she was exposed. Some in the clan seemed to gun for her, hoping she'd mess up and be permanently shunned.

Some things she no longer tried to hide. From the fact that she wore human clothing to the fact that she would not choose a mate, she was considered "gall" or undesirable. The Overseers tried for a time to bend her to their will, but it only succeeded in frustrating them. If it wasn't for Arn, she was sure she would have been exiled from the clan or thrown down the endless pit in the furthest part of the Siege.

The sin that brought her current penance was something she held so precious that she'd never apologize or recant being involved with.

Liberia, a female her own age, discovered that Serena hid deep in the woods, with, of all things, a book! A human book. Liberia was all too happy to report it to the Overseers. Serena was brought before the council and grilled on everything from how she knew how to read to where the book had come from. There was no way she was going to tell them Arn taught her to read and even more disastrous, that a human had actually given the book to her.

Serena stood before them and didn't utter a word, and in return, she was beaten and exiled to the cabin until such time as she revealed it all or served her time in full. Before she left, bloodied and weak, they burned her book before her eyes. She watched as it went up in flames, and it was the only time during the whole ordeal that she almost cried. The loss of the book was worse than all the bruises and cuts she carried.

Arn was held captive as she was driven from the Siege, items being hurled at her as she was called all kinds of unspeakable things. But she held her head high as she walked away.

That was almost three months ago, and with fall setting in, she needed to decide if she was going to try to go back or not. She wasn't sure what to do, but one thing she knew for sure, she'd never reveal Arn or Vivienne's involvement. They were two people who meant the world to her, and she'd protect them at all costs.

Serena was pulled from her reverie by a red pickup truck parking near the edge of the lot. Its lights went black and the engine shut off. Whoever it was waited. Serena paused to make sure that it was only Jack and no other.

She could make out his silhouetted form through the window. He tapped his fingers on the steering wheel, looking around expectantly.

Taking a deep breath, she dropped from the tree and moved toward the vehicle. She was so excited her heart was fluttering like a butterfly in her chest. In moments, he'd be within reach.

Before she broke through the forest line, she forced herself to calm and not run to the truck. He shouldn't see her so anxious to be in his presence.

Reaching the driver's side, she tapped on the window. His eyes turned toward her, and even in the faint light, they appeared bright. A smile spread across his face as he lowered the window.

"Serena." Her name on his lips sounded like a plea. She wanted to hear him say it over and over again. She wondered if she could.

"Hello, Jack." A blush stole across her face and she lowered her gaze. Remembering she was out in the open, she motioned for him to exit the car. No matter how dark it was, they needed to move. "Come, we need to go into the woods, not far, but enough to stay hidden."

"Okay." Jack nodded and got out, carrying a bag. As he made

his way, he glanced around nervously. She wanted desperately to know what he was thinking.

About twenty feet into the woods, she stopped to face him. "So, how are you? Is your wound healing?"

As she turned to Jack, she almost jumped in surprise. He was right there, within inches of her. Her heart pounded so loudly, she was sure he must hear it. His body radiated warmth, and she welcomed it. More than that, she wanted it like she wanted to breathe.

Her conscience was telling her this was wrong, and how dangerous it was, but all she could do was stare at his mouth and gaze up into his shadowed eyes.

"How are you, Serena? I've been worried about you. I was hoping you hadn't gotten into trouble with your own kind. I just had to see you were all right."

Serena smiled, thrilled at his concern. "I was already in trouble with my clan." It was heady that he'd actually thought about her.

Jack's eyebrows rose. Serena lifted her hands in reassurance. "No, don't worry, they know nothing about you. It's safe." He nodded and seemed to relax.

She watched in wonder as his free hand came up and trailed down her face, slowly, softly, and seductively. She resisted the urge to throw herself into his arms. His touch left a blaze on her skin, like flames from a fire. As a Shilund, allowing a human to touch her this way should have felt wrong, but it was utterly and completely right to every part of her yearning cells.

"Your skin is as soft as I thought," Jack said almost to himself. He studied her intently, and skimmed his fingers across her cheek with a feather-light touch. Using his thumb, he brushed her lips gently, his eyes fixated on them. "Your mouth is beautiful."

Serena blinked once, then again, and then once more. No one had ever called her beautiful. It was funny how special it made her feel. She wanted to say something, but the hypnotic gaze of the strikingly handsome human male rendered her speechless.

She looked into his light blue eyes and seemed to get lost. Her thoughts jumbled. This must be what it was to be attracted to someone. This was so new, so perfect, and it left her slightly giddy. Without thinking, she wrapped her arms around him, gently laying her head against his chest. His heart was beating so fast. She wondered if she was affecting him in the same way he was affecting her.

She trailed her hands up his muscular back and his arms

responded by wrapping around her, cradling her, pressing her to him. This was where she belonged. In her whole life, she'd never felt like she belonged anywhere. But here...right now...with his arms around her, this was perfect.

"I suppose you are happy to see me, too?" Jack quipped as he rubbed her back.

"Yes, I am, Jack. I am extremely happy to see you," she breathed. It was true. This was the most happiness she had ever experienced in her entire life.

His lips pressed against her head in a kiss. "Hey, I brought you something," he said as he pulled away and held up the bag.

"What is it?" she asked with a smile.

He chuckled. "Well, open the bag and find out."

Serena took the bag and opened it. She withdrew an article of clothing and unfolded it. It was a soft, pink sweater in her size. It was thick, and she loved it immediately.

"You got this for me?" She could not hold back the disbelief in her voice as she stood holding it out and marveling at it. It was all so unexpected.

"Well, I noticed that your sweater, the only sweater I've ever seen you wear by the way, had holes in it. I thought you might like a new one. I also thought pink might look good with your dark hair."

It was for her. Only her. She was in awe. This human male gave her a gift. She was at a loss for what to say and thank you didn't seem like enough. She put the sweater back in the bag, and then reached around her neck, took off her necklace, and handed it to him.

It was impulsive, rash, and if anyone in her clan saw her, she would be thrown down into the pit. She was committing an unforgivable sin, but she didn't have it in her to stop. This was the right thing.

He stared down at his open palm at the pewter symbol in awe. It was an intricately twisted set of shapes that made up one stunning whole. He held it up and studied it intently.

"I have had this my entire life. Now I want you to have it. It is one of the few things I own." She failed to tell him it was evidence of her lineage and her rights within the clan. Every Shilund had one, and it was proof to other clans as to one's identity and where one came from.

He regarded it again before looking back at her. "But I can't accept this. I can't. This is so much more than a sweater." He attempted to give it back.

"Please don't reject my gift, Jack. It is something I hold most dear. Please, accept this."

"I don't know..."

"Take it. Please," she pleaded.

What she offered him was of her. He didn't realize that, in her clan, giving her lineage was a covenant with another. He wouldn't understand it, but she was compelled to give it to him nonetheless as a promise. No one else in her clan would ever get it, no matter how hard the Overseers tried to push her to Rahfey.

A thrill shot through her as he took the necklace and put it around his own neck. She could see it resting against the dusting of hair at the juncture of his buttoned shirt. His fingers traced over it.

"Thank you, Serena. I'll cherish it always."

Serena nodded and stared at her feet. He would have no way of knowing what she'd given him. He would think it a trinket and nothing more. She knew where she wanted her commitment to be, and it was with the tall, dark-headed man who stood before her.

As she beheld him, he grew closer, and before she could say anything, he reached down, lifted her chin, and kissed her. It was a soft kiss at first, and then it progressively became needy and deep. A jolt of electricity surged through her like every part of her cells was on fire. She was quicker to embrace him this time, wrapping around him to get as close as possible.

He smelled sweet, like the fresh moss on the bank of the creek that ran below the Siege entrance. His taste was unlike anything she had ever known, and she wanted more. His tongue met hers, and though she should be alarmed, she wasn't. It was heavenly, and she wanted more and more of him. His hands trailed down her back, pulling her closer if that were even possible. Her purring began and she didn't even try to fight it.

Jack broke the kiss, touched his forehead to hers, breathing heavily. "Serena..." He trailed off as he panted. "That sound you're making...I hope it means you like this."

She smiled. "That is exactly what it means. But, why did you stop? I found it very ...pleasant," Serena whispered, eyes closed, his breath warming her lips.

"I think I need to slow down," he replied hesitantly as he exhaled. "God, you taste good."

She opened her eyes to gaze into his. "I like how you taste, too."

He leaned in and softly brushed his lips against hers. "I've been dreaming about doing that since we last said goodbye."

She gave him a smile right as his phone rang. Frowning, he glanced down at it.

"Hello? Yes. It's my day off. Can't you...? No. No, of course. I'll be right there." He hung up and hugged her tight. "I'm being called in, I have to go."

Serena's heart sank. She didn't want him to go, not for anything.

"Can I see you again?"

She knew she should say no, but nothing was going to keep her from him. Not her clan, not their differences—nothing. "Yes, I want to see you again too."

Jack smiled. "Call me when you can meet. I'll be waiting."

He kissed her forehead then started making his way out of the woods, looking back every few seconds and smiling at her.

Just before breaking through the trees, he paused. "Just don't keep me waiting long."

She giggled. A sound she hadn't made since she was very small. "I won't."

Seemingly satisfied, he turned and headed toward his truck.

She was giddy until he drove away, and then a sudden bereavement claimed her. Her body still tingled at every point he'd touched. What was this human male doing to her? She was completely entranced and wanted more time with him. Sighing, she knew she would have to wait patiently until their next meeting.

When his taillights faded over the small ridge, she reluctantly turned to head to the cabin.

Little did she know, they had not been alone in the woods.

Chapter 14: Jack

Leaving Serena was the hardest thing Jack had done in a long time. He had glanced back in his rearview mirror, hoping to see an image of her somehow as he drove away. But that didn't happen; she was lost in the darkness of the woods.

He didn't know why, but he couldn't fight the fierce need to protect her. He knew she could take care of herself as she had been, but that didn't seem enough. She needed him or maybe, he needed her. He needed to know she was safe, and knowing that Rahfey character was out there left him completely on edge.

He toyed with the necklace, fingering the symbol, tracing its outline and smiling. He knew she had given him something important. Maybe she liked him too. He knew she at least cared for him in the way someone was expected to when they saved another's life—the desire to see them live and thrive. But to think she had the same sort of attraction to him brought things into sharp perspective. She was what he wanted, as bizarre as it was. She was not human, and he was not even sure how compatible their species were, but he wanted to try, without a doubt. He would figure something out.

Making his way back into town, he pulled into a service station to fill up his truck. It was a busy store, as most folks stopped to fill up or to buy beer there. As he pulled out the nozzle to fill his truck with gas, he noticed a dark-haired stranger in a black t-shirt and fatigues, speaking to Tom inside. Jack watched intently as Tom appeared to be giving the man directions, pointing here and there.

He shook Tom's hand and exited the store as Jack finished pumping gas. The man got into a black SUV and as it turned to exit the lot, he noticed "Fringe Hunters" emblazoned on the side. The vehicle disappeared down the road.

Jack made his way inside the small store. Tom leaned against the counter.

"What was that all about?"

Tom shrugged his shoulders. "Some Bigfoot hunter or something. He was asking about the national park, and how far away the Canadian Forestry border was. He didn't really say why. He bought a map and took off."

Jack nodded. "Great."

He remembered the show *Fringe Hunters* from one of the cable networks. They searched around the country looking for any type of oddity, like aliens and electrical vortexes. He was immediately uneasy.

"Hey, Jack?" Tom questioned while Jack put his card into his wallet.

His eyes shot up. "Yeah?"

"I'm really sorry about Chris and Adam. You, too, for that fact. But they were a damn shame. Really good guys." Tom's expression was sincere.

It was all Jack could do not to bolt out the door. His chest tightened, and he squeezed out, "Thanks, Tom."

"Tell their families for me if you see them, would ya?" Tom asked as the door dinged, indicating another person had just walked in.

Jack nodded once and then rushed to get back to his truck so he could get out of there.

Chapter 15: **Devon**

Devon Hennessey hated small towns. With all their dreary nothingness, most were hailed as a perfect spot to live. He scoffed at the thought. Small towns were the very essence of exposure, and he hated that. Driving through Presque Isle, Maine, he felt like a million eyes were watching him. He reassured himself that he would be out of this Podunk town soon enough.

He just needed to get the story and get out.

The one thing he knew to be an absolute truth was that even with small towns appearing so transparent, the surrounding areas typically held tantalizing secrets, ones he could not wait to find. Some of the freakiest stuff came from the most tiny, idyllic towns.

He drove to the other side of the city and pulled up to the Hideaway Hotel to check in. He knew his cameraman wouldn't be far behind, but he couldn't wait for him to get there. It wasn't like his last, larger production crew, but one cameraman would do.

In the meantime, Devon planned to start running down the strange posts that appeared on the show's blog a few months back, claiming an unknown humanoid creature was in the surrounding woods. Recently, the anonymous posters amped up the game by alleging the deaths of two firefighters were actually the work of those creatures.

His producer was all too willing to allow him to come to this lost little town to run down the story, and he was glad. Devon's last foray, searching for a credible sighting of Bigfoot, didn't yield anything but poison ivy. What a huge disappointment that had been. Not to mention, it made him look like a royal ass to the film crew. It had been a lot of conjecture and speculation that led absolutely nowhere. Well, this time was going to be different. He truly believed this trip was going to change his life.

He stood in the open door of the room, a reject from the sixties, all bright flowers and strange patterns. There was a double bed, a TV with rabbit ears sitting on top, a beat-to-hell dresser, and a push-button phone that had seen better days. No matter, he wasn't going to be here long.

After lugging his bags into the rented room, he slammed the door with his foot and hefted everything onto the bed, the dense bags falling on the mattress with a bounce. Relieved to be starting down the path of being settled, he focused on what it would take to begin his work. Work was good. Distraction was better. He pulled out a loaded gun from the back of his pants and chambered a round, laid it down on the bathroom sink within close reach, and made sure the door was locked.

As he wandered into the bathroom, he stopped at the mirror and took a good look at himself. The dark circles under his eyes were more pronounced, and his skin was a bit weathered. Since he rarely looked at himself in the mirror, changes to his appearance always took him by surprise. Even the wrinkles around his eyes had deepened, too much for a man of twenty-six. Well, he felt ancient, so it seemed to fit.

With his hand, he rubbed the stubble on his face and thought a shower and a shave would be good. A shower always made him feel clean and reborn. Maybe this time the illusion of clean would hold, and he would forget who he was and what he had done. But no matter what he did to rinse off his shame, his past always found a way to rear its ugly head. And no matter how he tried to change, the stamp of the military life was never going away. He was set in a mold that he couldn't break.

He undressed and stepped under the stream of water, keeping the curtain open in order to watch the door if anyone should happen to come in. That way he could make it to the gun before they reached him.

Once showered, he sat on the bed with a towel wrapped around his waist, taking out an apple and a folder from his bag. Lying back against the headboard, he took a bite of his red delicious and began reading the coroner's reports of the deaths of Chris Jenkins and Adam Hensley.

Chapter 16: Arn

Arn had just made it into the Siege with two rabbits in hand when he found Baden waiting with Rahfey, looking like they wanted to speak to him. He hoped they had no idea that he had gone by the cabin to check that Serena was okay, even though she had been nowhere in sight.

Arn pushed past them, handed off the catch to a nearby male, and walked determinedly toward the tunnel that led to his small corner of the Siege. The main part of the cave was a vast open area with tunnels that jutted in different directions, lit up by various torches and battery-powered lights. He wasn't sure where Baden or the Overseers got the batteries, and he never wanted to ask.

As he entered his space, footsteps behind him indicated that they had followed him in.

Arn and Serena's area was compact, with two beds, a small table, and various oil lanterns. It was lined with shelves all around. Arn busied himself with lighting the oil lamps, hoping that by ignoring them, they would go away.

"Arn," Baden's deep voice boomed. "Serena's penance will be over at the next full moon."

Arn didn't want to talk to Baden about this. "This is news why?" He went about straightening up his area so that he didn't have to stop and look at them. If they saw he was busy, maybe they would take the hint. He could tell by their posture they weren't going anywhere. He wanted to curse under his breath.

"The Overseers have selected her mate, and when she returns, she'll be offered to him."

Arn's head whipped up, anger alight in his eyes. "What? Why would you do that now? Can't you allow her to return and try to re-assimilate into the clan? Why put that on her before she's even had a chance to return?"

Baden was a tall male, but he didn't tower over Arn like he did most, and even though he was big, his body was soft from lack of use. His mouth was the only muscle he exercised now. "Her assimilation is precisely why I agree with them that it is time. The Overseers believe—"

"You believe," Arn corrected.

Baden smiled condescendingly through his blond, bushy beard. "The Overseers believe that her being forced outside of the community is not good and that if she were mated, this would allow for more acceptance with them."

"Right," Arn spat as he drew closer to stare into Baden's green eyes. "You just want her controlled. What better way to do that than to use a mate to do so?"

"Perhaps a mate will do better to corral her than you have been able to."

Arn fought not to punch Baden in the face. He knew if he did, it would be a direct challenge to his leadership, and he didn't want to do that. But he wasn't going to sit here and let them mate Serena to someone. Arn turned his eyes to Rahfey.

Then it hit him. *Of course, that's it.* Rahfey had long since been trying to get Serena to mate him and had even put in a formal request with the Overseers. But the last time Serena denied him, risking to be known as "gall," rather than to be mated to him. So, if he couldn't have her willingly, he would take her forcibly. Arn fought the urge to wrap his hands around Rahfey's neck.

"Rahfey, I would not have expected this from you. You say you love her, you've told me plenty of times that you do, and yet, you'll force her into a union with you? How is that love?"

Rahfey straightened his shirt, ran his hand through his long, light brown hair, and stood tall, looking Arn directly in the eyes. "Yes, I love her, and it is out of this love for her that I do this. I will make a good mate for her."

Arn chuckled. "And you think she'll just go along with this? Do you even know her?"

"I know if she doesn't do this, she could be lost forever to us, and I don't want that. Do you?"

Rahfey spoke with conviction and Arn could hear it. Maybe he did love her. But this wasn't the right way, and Arn would never ask her to do anything she didn't want to.

"Rahfey, this won't work. She'll never do this."

"She'll do it if you ask her to," Baden replied. "If you ask her as her father, she'll agree."

Arn was taken aback and laughed in a hard burst. "You want me to ask Serena to do this willingly? You sorely overestimate my influence on her. You said it yourself, I can't control her." *And I wouldn't want to.*

Baden walked around, picking up different items to study and then moving on. "I don't think so. I think you have a lot more influence than you let on." Baden stopped and faced Arn. "Which is why you'll ask her. If she doesn't agree to this, she will be an outcast for life, alone with no clan and never able to return. Further, we'll send word to other clans that she is gall. Do you understand?"

Arn stared at the both of them. What Baden said didn't even faze Rahfey. Well, he was showing his true colors now. Rahfey was willing to let Serena be pushed out forever, and he didn't even seem remorseful. Arn wanted to beat the living daylights out of each of them. He stood heaving, full of fury while they exuded calm.

They believe they have the upper hand. Maybe they do. But they are stupid if they think I'm going to help them.

"I'll leave it to you, Arn." Baden stared pointedly at Rahfey and slowly ambled out. Rahfey stood, as cool and collected as ever.

Arn moved closer to the younger Shilund. "Why, Rahfey? Why? Can't you respect her decision? If she doesn't love you, why do this?"

"She's sullied. By a human," Rahfey said matter-of-factly.

Arn stopped, surprised he knew about the human male, a fact Arn had only just stumbled upon himself this morning in the woods by the Dairy Queen. Arn had been drawn by Serena's scent as he hunted and followed her once finding she wasn't near the cabin. He watched in shock as Serena kissed the human male. It had troubled him, but he would talk to Serena about it when the opportunity arose.

"How do you know this?"

Rahfey cleared his throat, fidgeted, and then met Arn's eyes. "Because I've seen them together."

"When?" Arn asked. He thought maybe Rahfey was fishing to see if it might be true. Arn knew there had been a human scent around the cabin but hadn't seen anyone. If Rahfey was only guessing, it was an incredibly accurate guess. "You have no proof," Arn challenged, hoping to deflect from the truth.

"You think I lie?" Rahfey scoffed. "Go on and ask her. Go out to the cabin and confront her. Once you see her face, you'll know I'm telling the truth."

Arn shook his head. "No one is allowed out there." Not that Arn hadn't snuck out there a few times to check and make sure she was okay, but he wasn't about to confess that to Rahfey, or anyone else for that fact. Arn would leave her food and little things to let her know her father had not forgotten her.

"I won't tell anyone. But go on; go see her. And once you do, you'll know as well as I do that her mating me will save her. It's the only thing that will."

When Rahfey turned and walked out, Arn all but collapsed on the bed as he turned it all over in his head. As much as he didn't want Serena with a human, he didn't want her with Rahfey even more. But a relationship with a human would not work. It never had before, and he couldn't see it happening now.

He had been worried over Serena before, now he was terrified for her.

Chapter 17: **Serena**

"He did what!" Vivienne's voice was so loud coming out of the cell phone that Serena had to pull it away from her ear.

"Do not shout; it hurts my ears," Serena playfully chided. She had to smile at Vivienne's excitement. She was so much more open with how she felt at any given moment and Serena loved that about her.

Serena sat on the lone chair in her cabin, lovingly fingering the pink sweater in her lap. She wanted to put it on, but she also wanted to look at it more. It was the most special thing anyone had ever done for her.

"I'm sorry, I just can't believe Jack did that. A new sweater, wow, he must really be into you."

"Into me?" Serena's brows furrowed.

"It means he really likes you," Vivienne clarified.

"Oh. Yes, I think so. I'm into him too, I think."

"Serena!" Vivienne whispered disbelieving. "You like a human male. That rocks!"

"Rocks?"

"*Ugh*! Serena, you have to learn some slang. You kill me sometimes!"

"Kill? I never—"

"It means 'frustrate!' Never mind. So, are you going to see him again soon?"

Serena thought for a moment about him wanting to see her again. "Yes, he said he'd wait for me to call him."

"Well, do it soon, okay? Hey, maybe we can double date sometime." Loud noises were in the background, and Vivienne's voice got soft and urgent. "Hey, I've got to go. Mr. Powell is probably having a coronary that I'm taking too long on my break. Love you, hon!"

"Goodbye," Serena said and hung up the phone. What was a *double date*? Human expressions were so confusing. She moved to her bed and reached over to place the phone in a hiding place on the wall. She had also stored a book Vivienne had given her to read there. It was *The Outsiders* by S.E. Hinton. She planned to start it tonight. Vivienne had reassured her it would give her insight into how humans were as segregated by class as the Shilunds were. Serena couldn't wait to read about the *greasers* and *socs*, as Vivienne had called them.

Only two more nights here and she could return to the Siege. She wasn't sure she wanted to. She had been here for three months, and it had grown on her. No Overseer challenging everything she did or others watching her every move. Here, she could read books and be whoever she wanted to be. There, she would be expected to be what they wanted her to. She had accepted long ago that she was different and complying with their expectations would be a betrayal of who she was.

She walked out onto the porch and sat on the uneven steps that creaked as she put her weight on them. The warm sunlight spilled on her face and pushed out all the cold feelings she had. She wanted to stay here forever. It was an impossible wish, but one she held onto just the same.

Really, she was faced with three choices. Go back and comply...never. Go back and try to get them to see her side...yeah, wouldn't happen. Or become a nomad. The word nomad seemed scary. It basically relegated you to being forever alone. No other clan would help you unless you swore fealty to them. All her choices seemed bad.

Sighing, she tilted her head back so sunshine could warm her face completely. She wanted to go home to Arn, but that would be her only reason for returning. She couldn't bear the thought of being cut off from him.

It angered her that she even had to consider leaving him, that her clan was unbending about things. He was her father, after all. But she accepted in a resigned way that she really only had one choice. She remembered Vivienne teaching her the expression *rock and a hard place*. Yes, it certainly was the sum of things.

Chapter 18: **Devon**

Devon Hennessey kicked around some rocks at the campsite. He was at the scene of the attack that took the lives of two firefighters. He studied the dense forest and the kaleidoscope of light filtering through the ceiling of leafy tree branches. The birds relentlessly serenaded them like an orchestra. The day was spectacular, not hot, but comfortable. Had Devon not been on a mission, he could have sat for hours in the glory that was the sun and relaxed his day away, being lulled to sleep by the crickets and bugs as they went on their way.

His feet crunched against the brush as he moved about, studying the ground for any signs of something amiss. His cameraman, Tom Jacobs, was a few yards away, methodically cataloguing the site with his camera. His transition glasses were perched up on his thinning hair to give him unfettered access to the camera's viewfinder.

Evidence at the campsite indicated there'd been a struggle and old blood showed up in large, brown patches—signs of the victims bleeding out. Devon studied the footprints all around the site and found little that would be useful. The recovery team had made a mess of the scene, traipsing up and down over everything. He wanted to growl in frustration.

Idiots!

Lifting his head, he studied the area surrounding the site, looking for any evidence on the trees or even on the nearby path. There must be something to indicate what really happened. This was no cougar attack, no matter what they said. He knew it was something more sinister, and that sounded like a secret needing to be revealed.

Devon's skin began to crawl, like he was being watched. He scanned the area again but didn't see anything except the vegetation swaying in the wind. His military training told him if someone was watching and they were diligent, they could hide easily enough.

"I think I got all I can," Tom huffed, frustrated. "Not much here. But at least it will be good to intro the show with."

Devon glanced to Tom and nodded. "Yeah, I agree. Seems that whatever evidence was here is gone now. The sheriff of Mayberry and Barney Fife sure made a mess." This muck up of the area was indicative of small town emergency responders. No sense of suspicion at all, so they didn't care what they did when they happened upon a supposed accident.

"I'm ready to head back, what about you?" Tom balanced the camera on his arm and waited.

Devon sighed hard. He couldn't see anything that was going to help. "Yeah, I'm ready. I got to talk to the sheriff and find the survivor of this attack. Hopefully, that will lead us somewhere."

Tom nodded and started off down the trail. Devon paused and glanced around one last time, hoping to see someone watching them. It was still just trees, so he turned and followed.

The whole drive back, Devon rubbed his lip and considered what could have happened to the firefighters and how the one had survived. There was a story here, he knew it. He just had to figure out how to prove it.

When they made it into town, Tom dropped Devon off at the Presque Isle Sheriff's Department. The small, pale brick building had seen better days. A large, unlit neon sign read "Police," and "Presque Isle Sheriff" was painted on the window, as if the first sign wasn't indication enough.

Walking in, he surveyed the room. A large counter split the space into two sections. The public section, which housed a few chairs for waiting, and the police section, which had two desks, one neatly piled with papers and clipboards and the other bare except for a desk blotter. Beyond the desks were a hallway and a door that read "Sheriff Mason Pike." Devon was about to slap the bell on the counter, when a tall, muscular deputy emerged from the hallway.

"Can I help you?" The young deputy couldn't be any older than twenty-three. He was blond, and his hair was shorn close to the skin on the sides and only slightly longer on the top. Pretty typical of police and military. Devon regarded him over and how his appearance was ordered and all business. He could relate to this man. When Devon met his eyes, he noticed they were the oddest shade of green he had ever seen. Probably contacts because no one's eyes were naturally that green. *I guess the man needed a little vanity.*

"Yeah, I was wondering if Sheriff Pike was available." Devon tapped his fingers on the counter nervously. It was a habit he hated, but he still did it a lot. It helped him focus.

"No, I'm sorry. He had a meeting over in Caribou today. Can I help you?"

Tap, tap, tap.

Devon stared at the man's golden name tag. Deputy Henry

Parrish.

"Well, Deputy Parrish, I was wanting some information on the attack that happened a few weeks back. The alleged wild cougar attack that killed two and wounded a third. Are you familiar with that?"

Deputy Parrish nodded blankly. "Yes, I am. What information are you needing?" The deputy rested his hand on his gun, not in a menacing way, but as someone who was so used to having the weapon strapped to him that it was like a part of his body.

Devon leaned down on his elbows. "I'm with the show *Fringe Hunters*, and we were interested in any photos of the bodies that were taken at the scene. And the report, if it's available."

Tap, tap, tap.

Deputy Parrish remained stoic, menace rolling off him. "I'm sorry, the only thing I can let you have is the public record, which is housed in those binders over there." He indicated a shelf with multiple notebooks, labeled by year.

Devon thought it was funny a three-inch binder was big enough to hold reports for a full year. This definitely wasn't the hub of criminal activity.

Devon stood and reached into his pocket, producing a fifty-dollar bill. He held it up in order for Deputy Parrish to get an eyeful of it and leaned back onto his elbows again, keeping the fifty within view.

"I know the public record, what I'm actually after are details not released to the public. Of course, we'd leave your name out of it completely, and this would be for your trouble."

Devon held the folded bill between his index and middle fingers, signifying he was giving it to Deputy Parrish.

An incredulous grin appeared on Deputy Parrish's face. "Do you mean to bribe an officer of the law? Because if you are, I'd have to arrest you, but that can't be what you mean by holding that bill out, right?"

Great. A by-the-books man.

Devon straightened up and put the money in his pocket. "*Ah*, I guess not. So, the only report I can see is in the binder?"

"Yes, sir. That is what we give the public."

Deputy Parrish's attitude made Devon want to punch his lights out, but he held it together to get to the lousy report. He didn't need to end up in jail. He strolled over to the notebook and dropped it onto the counter with a thud. This made Deputy Parrish smirk. Shaking his head, the deputy walked back to the neat desk and sat down. While he worked, he kept periodically looking over at Devon.

Devon cursed to himself as he searched out the report in the book. Oh, there it was, right between a car that ran off the road and a loud noise complaint. *Geez.*

Reading the report, he noticed the names had been whited out. That sucked. Then it occurred to him to look on the back, and sure enough, he could make out the names showing backward. As slowly as he could, he took out a piece of paper and a pen and wrote down the letters.

JACKSON DAY

Hmm. He'd have to find this Jackson Day and see what he could tell him. But in the meantime, he should get a copy of this report.

He pulled it out and waved it at the fine deputy. "Do you think I could get a copy?"

Deputy Parrish got up. "For ten cents."

"Ten cents, *huh?* Wouldn't happen to have change for a fifty, would you?"

Deputy Parrish opened his mouth to say something. Devon immediately held up his hand to interrupt him. "No, I don't suppose you would. Well, here's a quarter. Keep the change."

The deputy took the sheet and the quarter and disappeared into the back. Devon figured he could go to the town diner and find out whom this Jackson Day person was. He had no doubts his interview was going to be crucial.

Deputy Parrish returned and handed him the copy and fifteen cents in change. Devon had to smile at the fine officer. He wouldn't even keep the change. Bet he never broke any rules, sped, or peed without putting down the seat. How boring.

Devon folded up the paper and shoved it into his pocket. Heading toward the door, he saluted the deputy. "Thank you, sir."

Once outside, he took in a good breath of air. He was relieved to have been out of there. Now to find Jackson Day.

Chapter 19: **Serena**

Serena was on cloud nine. She and Jack had spoken on the phone three times since they last met, and she was thankful for the gift of the phone. Vivienne had known exactly what she needed. It was quickly becoming a lifeline to Vivienne and Jack. Why would Shilunds be against this kind of thing?

Jack had told her so many details about himself. He fought fires for a living, had a sister who had died young, and liked something called board games. She found him to be kindhearted and gentle in his speech patterns and that made her attracted to him all the more.

As they talked, she yearned to be near him, to touch him, and to smell his masculine scent. Maybe even kiss him again, if he'd allow it. They decided to meet again in two days' time. Same time, same place. She could hardly wait.

Walking around her cabin, she hugged herself in her pink sweater. She only allowed herself to wear it here so she wouldn't get it dirty when she hunted or walked to see Vivienne.

Her phone gave off a warning beep, indicating the battery was running down. She powered it off and plugged it into the charger. But the charger didn't have much charge left either.

She'd have to find a place to recharge it soon. Maybe the Remery Textile Mill, which sat on the edge of town. It did have some external plugs. Maybe she could sneak there tonight and use one.

A soft knock sounded on her door, which made her jump. Who could be here? She rushed to her hiding place, placing the phone and charger inside, walked to the door, and opened it, only to see Arn about ready to knock again.

Arn smiled at her. "I was beginning to think you weren't here."

"Hello, Papa," Serena said, and leaned in to hug him. He was taller than her so she fit right under his arms. She laid her face against his chest. "I've missed you." She pulled back as Arn's mocha eyes inspected her. She gave a wry smile. "Although, I knew you were always close by. Your gifts told me. Come in before someone sees you."

Serena pulled him in and quickly searched around. Seeing no one, she shut the door.

Arn's presence seemed to fill the entire cabin. Serena smiled and walked around the table. "What are you doing here? I'm technically not off penance until tonight at the full moon. Do you want to accompany me back?"

She hoped that was not the case. She wanted to try to go to the textile mill. If he were here, she would not be able to go.

Arn shook his head and frowned. "No, nothing like that." He turned to her and sighed. Looking her over, his frown deepened. "Where did you get that sweater?"

Serena smoothed it. "I got it out of the thrift shop bins. I liked it and thought if the humans were giving it away, it would be okay to keep it." She hoped he wouldn't sense her lie.

Arn nodded, and Serena let out an inward sigh of relief.

"So, why are you here?"

"Can't a father see his only daughter?" Arn chuckled, and then relented. "No, you're right. I had a purpose in coming here. I need to tell you something before you return."

His troubled expression made her very uncomfortable.

"What is it?" she whispered.

"The Overseers...they have announced Rahfey as your intended."

Serena stared into Arn's eyes as she dropped into the chair. This couldn't be happening.

No! No! NO!

"What?" Serena wanted to hurt something. Why were they doing this to her? She did not want Rahfey and had denied his request several times. He knew she did not want to mate him. It was one thing to deny him, and another thing to deny the order from the Overseers and the Anaximander.

"I'm sorry, Serena. I'm not sure when they decided it, but they came to me and told me to expect it when you returned. You'll have no choice, and they expect me to talk you into it."

"Did Rahfey have anything to do with this?"

Arn sighed and sat on the bed, resting his arms on his knees. "I'm not sure when he knew what or when he became involved in this, but he certainly knows."

Serena's heart sank. She didn't want this to happen. She wanted control of her life, to be able to choose her mate and live, as she desired. She did not want to be forced into mating someone she had no feelings for, only to fulfill a stupid mandate of the Shilund to mate and produce offspring.

She wanted to be human.

Humans chose their mates and how to live their lives. Some chose never to propagate the human race. But that was okay in their society. If they decided their mating wasn't working, they had recourse to choose a new mate instead. Not like the Shilund who demanded it be for life. Arn had always told her to mate for feeling and not for expectation. He was adamant about it and when he talked of the decision, he always seemed in some pain.

Beyond all of that, she wanted Jack. She admitted to herself that it was too soon for her to feel like that. But still, that was who she wanted to be close to, who she had feelings for. Arn would understood that much, but the "human" thing might be more than he could take.

"I won't mate Rahfey," Serena said bluntly. "I won't. I know what I risk, but I cannot be joined to him."

Arn sighed. "Are you sure, Serena? He would try to be a good mate to you. Could you not try?"

"There is no trying, Arn, and you know it. Once joined to him, I will not have a life. Who I am will be forfeit."

Arn stood and came close to her. "If you don't join with him, you will definitely be outcast. There is no maybe to it. Those are your only options."

Serena fought the threatening tears. This was unfair and uncalled for. How dare the Overseers try to dictate her life? She should have autonomy over whom she mated, and where and how she lived. But they did not want that to happen.

"I will not mate him. I know what I risk." Serena gazed up at him.

A myriad of emotions crossed his face. He was struggling, and she knew it. He pulled her up into his arms.

"I know you are not mine by blood, but I love you as my own. I do not want to lose you."

"You won't," she whispered against his shirt. "No matter what happens, you will never lose me."

Arn rubbed her back and whispered, "I hope you're right." He pulled her back to look into her eyes. "And no matter what you decide, I'll support you and stand by your side."

Serena shook her head to protest, but Arn silenced her. "Hush now, it's settled. I'll see you later tonight when you return."

Arn kissed her head and turned to leave, his footsteps heavy. Before he departed through the open door, he paused. "Serena?"

"Yes?"

"Is there anything else you want to tell me? I mean about your time here in the cabin?" he asked slowly, eyes boring into hers.

There really was only one other thing she could tell him. It involved the dark-haired human she couldn't get out of her mind and heart. She could tell him, but instead, she shook her head. "No. Why?"

His expression became wistful. "Nothing." He gave her a brief smile, winked, and disappeared into the day.

Serena sat down and cried, knowing things were about to get ugly very fast. She could run away and never look back. But she couldn't do that to Arn. No, she'd face this head on and hope she made it through alive.

Chapter 20: Jack

The warm, sunny day provided the perfect opportunity for the Presque Isle Fire Department to wash their massive engines. They did one at a time in case of an alarm. You wouldn't know they were adults used to wielding large hoses in a very controlled manner, because being around water hoses and soap made all the men behave like children. Someone getting squirted here, soaked pants there, and of course, a soapsuds crown for someone. No matter how mature someone was, when it was their turn to rinse with the hoses, you better watch out. Someone else always got wet.

Jack was still on restricted duty, but nothing was going to keep him from being in the middle of this. Restricted duty didn't say anything about not being allowed to wash a truck. Of course, he was the worst offender on the hoses.

He had just finished hosing down Mac Bray, when a man moving like a soldier and wearing army pants and a black shirt walked up to watch the snickering chaos. He stood there for a moment, taking it all in with a menacing glower. Jack knew immediately that it was the man he saw at the gas station not too long ago. But he made no move to greet him.

"I'm looking for Jackson Day. I hear he works here," he yelled above the laughter.

All the firemen stopped their horseplay and stood frozen, glaring at the man. Brad Likins was the first to acknowledge him. "Who wants to know?"

The man shifted his weight slightly and held out a business card. "I have to speak with him. Is he here?"

Brad walked up, took the card, and studied it suspiciously. "*Fringe Hunters?*"

"Yes. I want to ask him a few questions about the attack that happened."

Everyone stiffened in response, and a profound sense of dread washed over Jack. This was a departmental wound he was talking about and not just something that had only happened to Jack. They had all suffered the loss of Chris and Adam, and they were not going to open up to a random stranger.

"Well, what if he doesn't want to talk to you? That stuff is private, maybe he—"

Jack interrupted him as he moved closer and lifted his hand. "It's okay, Brad. I'll talk to him."

The man's whole body turned toward Jack. He smiled a devious grin, which immediately made Jack think of being a trapped animal. Well, too late now, he'd have to talk to the man. Maybe he could keep it brief.

"You sure? Me and the guys, we could—" Brad began.

"No, it's okay. Really, thanks, man." Jack patted Brad on the back. Brad nodded, handed Jack the card, and joined the rest of the guys.

Jack read the name and knew the mysterious logo.

Devon Hennessey
Host,
Fringe Hunters,
New York, New York.

Jack tapped the card on his hand and regarded the man. "What can I help you with, Mr. Hennessey?"

Devon smiled again. "Is there somewhere we can talk? Somewhere a little less...sunny?"

"Sure, there is a picnic table on the side of the building. We can sit there."

Devon nodded his assent and indicated Jack lead the way. Jack steered them to a homemade picnic table, which was situated under an overhang.

Jack sat down and Devon took the position across from him.

"So, what's this about?"

Jack asked the question but he already knew. He was aware of the reputation of the show, and how they went after anything paranormal. The show was gunning to find out about the Shilunds, he was sure of it.

"I'm interested in talking to you about the attack that killed your friends Chris Jenkins and Adam Hensley."

"I've already told the police all I know, which so happens, wasn't much. I passed out."

Devon smiled politely. "Yes, Mr. Day, I've read the report. However, in my experience, I know that people remember details well after the incident, details that don't always make it into the report. I was hoping you might have remembered more now that some time has gone by."

"I hate to disappoint you, but I honestly don't know what happened out there." *At least, not anything I would ever tell you.*

Devon nodded, doubt written all over his face. "So, where were you for all those days after the incident? You apparently showed up in town alive and with a bandage on your injury. It was even sewn up, evidently."

All the blood drained from Jack's face and he frowned. "Where did you hear that?"

The man must have paid someone in the hospital for details. The sheriff never once asked him about it to Jack's relief. He wasn't even sure that had made it into the report. The sheriff had quipped how lucky it was for Jack to have had a first aid kit to take care of himself. Jack had never disagreed with his wrong guess.

Devon shifted his weight and smiled an accusing grin. "Not everyone in a small town is able to keep their mouth shut."

"Especially when paid to talk," Jack countered. "I'm sorry you came all this way to ask me about a cougar attack." Jack rose to his feet. "Now I have to get back to work." He wanted to be as far away from this man as possible.

"Is that what it was?"

Jack stopped and faced Devon. "What?"

"A cougar attack. Was it a cougar that killed your friends?" Devon stared at Jack with expectancy.

Jack's whole body seemed stuck in place. "So they tell me." Jack forced himself to be as casual as possible and started toward the front of the firehouse.

"Well, I aim to find out for sure, Mr. Day. You can count on it!"

Jack could hear him yelling as he continued to walk away. He'd protect Serena at all costs, so he took the statement to heart.

Chapter 21: **Serena**

Serena greeted the sunset with mixed feelings. In one way, she welcomed it, because she needed the cover of night to go charge her battery pack. But she also hated the arrival of sunset for she'd be expected at the Siege. She didn't want to go there, but for Arn, she would attempt to be embraced back into the clan. But under no circumstances would she mate Rahfey. She'd make that abundantly clear to them and hope for the best.

She sat on the loading dock at the Remery Textile Mill, her feet dangling off the side as she waited patiently for the charger to get some charge. She gazed up at the sky and wished Jack was with her. It gave her some comfort to think about him being out there, under the same sky.

Once her battery pack was charged, she powered on her phone and found a waiting text from Jack.

Thinking of you tonight. Please be safe. She read the message and smiled.

I will. Things will be okay. I will text you later.

I'm counting on it.

Taking a deep breath, she fulfilled a promise to call Vivienne before she made the journey to the clan.

Vivienne answered on the third ring. "Hey, Rena!"

"Hey, Viv."

"How you doing? Aren't you heading back to your peeps tonight?"

"Peeps?" Serena was confused. What was a peep?

"Your people, you know...what did you call them...your clan?"

"Oh yes, I am heading back to my peeps, as you call them." Serena's palms were sweating so much she almost couldn't hold onto the phone. "Vivienne, I'm not sure what is going to happen tonight, so I just wanted to call you and thank you. You've been the best friend I have ever had—"

"Why are you talking like you are going to be executed tonight?" Vivienne asked in a high, tight voice. "I can come and get you right now. I'm not sure where I could take you, but you don't have to go back to face death. Because that is how you just sounded. Like you are facing death."

Because I just might. "I don't think it will be that serious, but still, I'm not sure what they will say. Probably nothing of consequence."

"Rena, you sound funny, I mean, even funny for you. Are you sure everything is okay?"

No. "Yes. Everything is fine. I promise. But I wanted to keep my oath to call you as you asked."

Vivienne began slowly, "Okay. If you say so."

Serena let out a strong exhale. "I'll call you tomorrow and let you know how things went, one way or another, okay?"

"Sure, Rena. And just know I am pulling for you. I mean, supporting you."

Serena rolled her eyes and smiled. She did know what that expression meant without Viv's explanation.

"Thanks, Viv. I'm glad you are. Now, goodbye."

Before Vivienne could respond, Serena hung up the phone. *Time to get this over with.*

Serena slowly made the journey toward the cave, letting the music of the night comfort her, from the hoot of the owl to the crickets keeping time to the bullfrog's lonely bellowing to others of its kind. How easy it was to be an animal in the forest. Their emotions greeted her, and it made her think how uncomplicated their lives were. They thought mostly like children, of simple things like food, warmth, shelter, or escaping a predator. Sometimes, but mostly they focused on survival. Kind of like her now.

After a time, she arrived at the foot of the hill that housed the cave in which her clan lived. She stopped and stared into the darkness. Adjusting her bag on her shoulder, she ascended up the hill. She could feel the eyes of the guards in the trees around her, watching and no doubt passing judgment on her. Sniffing the air, she recognized who was there. They didn't like her, and the feeling was mutual.

She dreaded what was coming, but was so glad Arn had let her know what to expect. Rehearsing the rejection speech she was going to give to the Overseers about the mating was what kept her sane long enough to pull back the ivy that hid the entrance. She tried to push Jack out of her mind, because thoughts of being separated from him almost brought her to her knees, and she couldn't afford to be weak now.

Coming through on the other side, she walked down the short, quiet tunnel until she reached a large opening. A fierce fire burned in the middle of the floor, and the smoke from it billowed and rushed out a tunnel at the top. Around it, males and females of her kind sat waiting, no doubt for her. When they spied her, all rose in quiet expectation. The eight Overseers stood to the left, hands poised in front of them, waiting. Before them, the ninth Overseer and the alpha, Baden, stood with Rahfey at his side.

The air almost crackled with the built-up tension in the room. Serena descended and strode forward to stand tall and proud in front of crowd, holding onto the strap of her bag, and defiantly meeting the gaze of all the eyes trained on her. There would be no bowing down, no repentance for the crime she was guilty of that had sent her to the cabin these lonely three months. And she would not bow down to the forced mating she knew was coming.

She made her way to the Overseers to present herself. She caught sight of Arn standing a few feet away, ready to embrace her as soon as it was over with. Serena gave him a small nod, and he winked in reply.

Stopping in front of Baden, she gazed up into his green eyes and noticed his lips were drawn tight, outlined by the furry beard that almost resembled a small animal attempting to jump off his face. She wondered idly how he kept food out of it.

Serena bowed slightly. "Rulers, I have done my penance as was required and request I be allowed fellowship into the clan once more."

No one said anything for a moment, and then the deep resonance of Baden's voice sounded out. "Serena, we do want to welcome you back into the fellowship of this place. However, only part of your penance has been paid."

There was murmuring among the gathered Shilund there.

Serena made no movement. *Here it comes.*

Her gaze shot to Arn. His face was unflinching. He gave her a supportive nod. She knew he would support any decision she made, no matter the cost.

Her heart hammered so hard in her chest she thought she might explode. Part of her wanted to run, but she forced herself to stand rooted in place. Her eyes turned to Rahfey. He had the nerve to smile at her. She merely frowned in response.

"I don't understand. My punishment was isolation for three months, which I have paid. No other requirement was requested."

Baden licked his lips and then spoke louder. "The Overseers understand that part of the issue of you fitting into the clan is the lack of a mate to help guide and steer you in a proper direction. As is our tradition, if a female of our kind has not made a selection by twenty years of age, a mate can be selected for her for the furtherance of our species."

I will not mate him. I would rather die first.

Serena forced her words out. "So I am required to be mated, as part of my penance?" She glared at Rahfey, who stood with his arms behind his back, staring at her

I wish I'd cut your throat when I had the chance.

Baden turned to look at the other Overseers. The Overseers appeared stern and calm, showing that they approved of what he said.

"Yes, Serena, we agree that this would be the best thing for you and for our clan. You not being mated has left you directionless and prone to lean toward detestable human things."

"Detestable? A book is detestable?" The question came out tighter than she had intended, and she knew it would be taken as a sign of disrespect. But, she didn't have any respect for Baden or the Overseers at the moment. Maybe she never had. They simply wanted to control her, and she'd never allow them or anyone to do that.

"See, she has been tainted by the human world." He waved his hands toward the group as if her reply was evidence of guilt. Murmurs rose behind her.

"Knowledge is a desirable thing. It makes us strong, and if we all strive for knowledge, we will be a strong clan. Why is it wrong to want to know things?" she challenged loudly. "If we knew more about the human world, maybe it would help us be better—"

"Enough!" Baden yelled, causing everyone to quiet. "We will hear nothing more about this." Baden turned toward Rahfey and urged him forward. Rahfey, the good boy he was, obeyed and stopped directly in front of her.

"This male, Rahfey, has been chosen as mate for you. The ceremony will be performed now in order for you to remain in this clan."

Serena glared into Rahfey's eyes. God, how she hated him right now. He disgusted her, and she knew her face showed it. But Rahfey solemnly held out his hand. She glanced down at it and shook her head.

"No," she said, loud enough for Rahfey to hear.

"Serena," he pleaded, leaning into her. "You must do this in order to return, or you will be worse than gall. You will be an outcast. Take me as mate and save yourself." He pushed his hand forward to try to take hers. Without thinking, she stepped back and spat on his shoes.

Rahfey was mortified, and the clan immediately started protesting. She had just shown Rahfey the most disrespect one Shilund could show another. Serena glanced over to Arn. Pain shone in his eyes, but he nodded in support.

"Striping! Striping!" some yelled as the Overseers talked animatedly to one another. Baden leaned back to speak to one of them and then turning back, he raised his hands.

"Silence!" he shouted, and it took a moment for everyone to finally quiet. Glaring at her, he spat, "Serena, you have disrespected your intended. This cannot pass."

"He is not my intended. I reject him as my choice." Serena fists clenched and she wanted to make them listen to her...

"Striping!" was chanted by more of the clan and again, Baden lifted his hands in order to silence them.

Baden turned to Rahfey. "Rahfey, your intended has disrespected you without cause, do you call the rite of striping as retribution?"

"He's not my intended!" Serena yelled, but Baden ignored her, waiting for Rahfey's answer.

Rahfey stared at her, and without even a change in expression, said, "Yes."

Hands yanked her away, and Arn began to yell. Someone held him back, and he struggled to be free, fighting each Shilund that came in contact with him. Serena tried to make sure Arn was okay, but wasn't able to see anything as she was forced toward the large oak beam at the end of the cavern. It had two iron rings at the top and restraints that dangled down. At the bottom were leg shackles to keep a person in place.

She knew what was coming, the rite of striping, which was being whipped until every part of your back looked like it had been put through a meat grinder.

"No!" she shrieked, fighting to get free but unable to. She could hardly hear her own voice above the chanting of the mob as she tried to get the crowd's attention.

They took her pack from her, discarding it, and started to put the shackles on her. The cold iron cut into her wrist, and she couldn't get a good breath. Panic gripped her.

"Please Rahfey, don't do this!" she pleaded over her shoulder, but she couldn't see him. She knew as the offended party, he'd be the one delivering the blows.

The shackles were placed on her feet, effectively locking her in place. White-hot fire ran all over her, part panic, part fury. She couldn't believe this was happening.

"Arn!" she screamed. She couldn't help it; she was afraid and hoped he could spare her this. He didn't reply, and she couldn't find him. Her arms blocked her line of vision, wrists cuffed to the aged wood overhead.

Suddenly, it became deathly quiet, which meant Rahfey must be behind her with the whip ready to dole out her punishment. She could hear the scissors being used to cut up her black sweater, and the cold air hit her back as they pulled it out of the way.

"Please, Rahfey, don't do this!" was all she was able to get out before the first blow connected. It was like claws digging into her back, ripping her open all the way down. Her legs buckled for a moment. But she managed to pull herself back up. She was not going to surrender to it.

But then another strike landed, and all thought left her mind. All that was left was searing pain all over her body. She clenched her mouth tightly so as to not cry out, but by the time the next blow hit, she couldn't help but scream, and she was losing the ability to support her own weight.

In those moments, she thought of Jack and how she knew she loved him. She forced her mind to remember his cool, blue eyes and dark eyelashes. She imagined him smiling at her.

Another blow.

She let her head drop forward against the wood because she could no longer hold it up. Something warm dripped down her legs. Was that blood? Finally, a voice was in her ear—Rahfey.

"Please don't make me do this. Concede," he whispered. "Please, Serena, I would make you a good mate, I promise. Please give me a chance."

Gathering as much strength as she could muster, she forced herself to stand in defiance. Turning her head as much as she could, she found she only had enough strength to see his hands. He was clenching the whip so strongly the leather creaked in response. Was he honestly trying to tell her he could be a good mate in the middle of whipping her raw?

She couldn't help it. She began to laugh, and she had to admit, she sounded like a lunatic. It bubbled out and echoed through the cavern. When she finally stopped cackling like a mad woman, she replied with one of her favorite human phrases.

"Go to hell." Even though the Shilund had no concept of hell per se, she knew he understood her response.

Rahfey quietly walked back to his prior position. Serena tried to prepare for the next strike, whispering, "Jack, Jack, Jack."

The next blow landed, and Serena mercifully passed out.

* * *

She was being moved, she could feel the jostling, but she couldn't open her eyes. Then, everything went black.

When she surfaced again, she was on her stomach, and someone was attending her back. She started to move, but hands came down, gently.

"Try to stay still."

Arn, it was Arn. He was alive and safe. Oh, thank goodness. Then she passed out again.

When she came to, all around her was quiet. Every inch of her was on fire as pain radiated from her back. She turned her head and found Arn's sleeping figure sitting against the wall. She was in their dwelling in the cave.

She rose up as quietly as she could, barely able to hold a cry from escaping her lips. Looking around, she saw her bag and one of Arn's jackets. She moved as quietly as she could, because she didn't want to wake him. It was such an effort to put on a shirt; it seemed to take an hour, and it hurt as it dragged down the wetness on her back. She fought to stay conscious, but the pain screamed through all rational thought. On her way to the door, she grabbed his jacket and a hat. She turned back to look at Arn one last time before she left.

She almost didn't recognize him. His eye was bulbous and bruised, and his lip was split. Dried blood dotted his hairline and along his face. He had battled hard. But at least he was alive. She watched him for a moment. His face was set in a grimace while he slept. She loved him so much, but she needed to leave. This was no longer a safe place for her.

She forced herself to turn away and prayed she wouldn't run into anyone. Trying to walk normal was exhausting. Sweat broke out over her forehead from the exertion. Every movement was like a knife in her chest. But she had to get out if she wanted to survive.

The main cavern was empty, as it must be close to morning. She made it out of the opening of the cave and paused to take a breath.

She steeled herself, needing to walk away without appearing injured or the guard would recognize her. She hoped that they did not catch her scent.

She slowly moved down the hill, bearing down to keep from yelling out. Nausea threatened to rise. Breathing in through her nose and out from her mouth, she was able to keep bile from bubbling up in her throat.

Once she knew she was clear of everyone, she allowed her legs to buckle and threw up. Lying on her side, she panted. She'd made it out of the clan's immediate territory. Relief washed over her. She just wondered if she'd be able to make it to the edge of the forest. Somehow, she had to.

Lying there, watching the trees rustle in the light wind, she saw him coming toward her in a jog. Alaric. His large gray form was flanked by two other wolves, a russet and white one and a black one. Their emotions hit her all at once.

Blood. Danger. Hurt? Alaric thought.

She hadn't keened, so how had he found her? She gazed at him and keened a soft affirmation. The wolf nudged her with his nose and sat beside her. Serena could feel him tell his soldiers "danger."

Her hand trembled as she reached out to Alaric and brushed his fur, but the wolf kept his eyes up, alert. She wanted to stand and his large body rose in response. Pulling herself up against his back, she made it to standing.

She reached a nearby tree, using it to brace herself while fumbling for the cell phone in her bag. Powering it on, she closed her eyes and leaned her head against the rough bark. The pain made it hard to think clearly.

Warmth licked up her hand. Alaric. Caressing his head, she wanted so badly to collapse and not move. But if she gave in to that desire again, she wouldn't get back up. Opening her eyes, she dialed Vivienne's number. It rang multiple times. After so many rings, Serena's heart sank.

Please answer. Please answer.

Finally, a groggy Vivienne answered. "Hello?"

At first, Serena couldn't speak, but she pushed out, "Viv, I need your help."

"What?" Vivienne was suddenly alert. "What's wrong?"

Serena panted. "I've been hurt. I need you to come get me. Can you do that?"

"Hurt, how?" Serena could hear the panic in Vivienne's voice. Something shuffled in the background, and Serena guessed she was jumping up out of bed.

"Please," Serena begged. "Can you come to the parking lot where I brought Jack?"

"Yes, I'm on my way," Vivienne promised before hanging up.

Serena hugged the tree, so it supported all of her weight, and breathed in and out slowly. One way or another, she was going to make it out of this forest.

Chapter 22: Vivienne

Vivienne frantically jumped up in her dark room and threw on some clothes. She wasn't even sure they were clean. But they were next to her bed and available. She accidentally banged into her bedpost and froze. She waited to see if she could hear any noise from her parents' room. When there was only silence, she put on her shoes, grabbed her keys, and quietly snuck out of her parents' house.

She climbed into her car, put it in neutral, and let go of the emergency brake, allowing the vehicle to roll down the long driveway. Once at the bottom, she finally turned it on and started down the road. Her heart pounded in her ears so loudly and she wanted to throw up.

It must be bad for Serena to call her for help. She couldn't imagine what had happened. Did a hunter mistake her for an animal and shoot her? Had she fallen and broken a bone? Her mind raced with all sorts of the possibilities as to what could have happened, including the potential of her own kind having hurt her.

She pulled out her phone and dialed the one person who could help her with this. The phone rang over and over again. Finally, a male voice answered.

"Yeah?" Jack answered.

"Jack Day, this is Vivienne Jamison, Serena's friend. Serena just called me, and she's hurt. I'm going to pick her up and I need your help."

"What happened?" he demanded, stronger and more awake.

"I don't know, but I'm picking her up at the parking lot where I met you. Do you remember where that is?"

"Of course I do," was his panicked reply. "I'm on my way."

They hung up, and Vivienne relaxed a little at the thought that he was coming. He was a firefighter, and no doubt, he could help. Plus, he was kind of Serena's boyfriend.

"Hold on, Serena. We're on our way," Vivienne said to no one in particular and hoped to God no police would be along the way to stop her.

As she drove, she remembered the first time she had met Serena, on a fateful late night not unlike this one. She had been driving too fast down a country road, missed a turn, and slid right into the Aroostook River. She quickly started sinking and water rushed into her car unabated. She panicked so much that she almost couldn't force her fingers to undo the seatbelt. The water had been so loud as it flooded in that her voice didn't even carry as she cried out for help. The level rose until it was over her head and in her mouth. In those last moments, she thought of her mom and her dad and what they would go through at her funeral. She also thought about the fact that she was still a virgin. That thought should have made her laugh, but sitting there in a car drowning, it was a sad statement on her life.

She had just accepted she was going to die when hands pulled her out. Vivienne had lain on the riverbank trying to suck in air when she got her first look at her shadowed guardian angel. Serena had risked her own life to save her.

After that night, they became the best of friends, regardless of the fact that Serena wasn't human. Vivienne knew the friendship wasn't traditional, but it didn't matter at all. Different wasn't bad.

Vivienne shook away thoughts of that night and hoped that unlike that night, Serena's life wasn't in danger.

Chapter 23: **Serena**

Serena stumbled unsteadily down the path, pausing multiple times to take a breath and keep herself from passing out. Each step was like a jolt to her body. *Thank God for trees*, she thought as she caught herself. Each time she stopped, she had to force herself to move again, cheering herself on to put one foot in front of the other. She reminded herself each step brought her closer to help.

Honestly, she wasn't sure what Vivienne could do, but maybe she could hide her somewhere. Or even let her stay in the back seat of her car. She needed to be anywhere but here. Vivienne was the only one she thought of that could help. She really wanted to reach out to Jack, but she didn't want him to see her like this. Plus, she'd never be able to explain it. Love him as she did, she wasn't sure he wouldn't understand. It occurred to her that Vivienne may not either.

She rubbed the edge of the jacket and thought of Arn, hoping he would gather what had happened. She didn't want to think about how he would react when he saw she had taken his jacket and hat and left. She prayed he wouldn't come looking for her anytime soon and would just accept that she needed to distance herself from the clan. If he tried to find her and bring her back, well, that could just get messy. It would put him on a collision course with Baden and the Overseers more so than he already was, and she didn't want him shunned. That he was ignorant of her leaving might be the only thing that would allow him to stay in the Siege. If they believed he helped her in any way, they might misconstrue that as being complicit. If she could just get away it would give him plausible deniability. She prayed he would read the subtle signs and let her retreat somewhere to heal and figure things out.

Her acute eyesight and hearing didn't pick up anything out of the ordinary as she shuffled along the path so she wasn't being followed, except by her wolf guards. But she needed to hurry in case Rahfey had looked in on her; he might realize she was gone and send someone to find her. Who knew how much influence he had over the whole of the clan?

At one point, she stopped and held onto a tree, not caring the prickly bark was biting into her face. She thought of Jack again. She could see him smiling and beckoning her along. It was a stupid fantasy, but pretending he was there with her somehow eased the pain.

It took forever to reach the parking area. Breaking through the trees, her heart stopped at what she saw. A truck and a car were in the lot. Vivienne was leaning against the car and a tall male was pacing. Her heart leapt when she saw it was Jack beside Vivienne, waiting for her.

He's here!

Something in her was so completely relieved that she gave into the pain and fell face-first on the ground. The last thing she remembered was of Jack and Vivienne rushing toward her and the patter of Alaric's paws as he ran away.

Chapter 24: **Jack**

Jack watched Serena fall in slow motion. Rushing to her was like trying to run through deep water. He just couldn't get there fast enough, the light of his flashlight jolting in every direction.

"Serena!" Vivienne yelled as she dropped to her knees beside Serena just as he did. She lifted her hand slowly off Serena's back and frowned.

"Why is she wet?" she asked as she held up her hand.

Jack was making sure he could feel breathing on his hand, which he did. Relief flooded him that she was alive. He angled his flashlight to illuminate her better and caught sight of Vivienne's hand.

His heart skipped a beat when he saw blood. He shined the flashlight on her back and noticed a burgundy stain on her jacket. Moving quickly, he lifted up the jacket and shirt to find her back torn to ribbons.

"Oh God!" Vivienne gasped, mirroring his feeling. "What happened to her back?"

"I don't know, but she's lost a lot of blood. I want to get this stitched up as soon as I can. It needs to be cleaned too so no infection settles in."

He picked her up as gently as he could and carried her to his truck, her blood seeping into his arms and shirt.

He couldn't figure out what had happened. What kind of an accident would cause those types of tears to her back? The only thing that came to mind was being whipped. His heart stuttered. Had her own people done this to her? She had planned to go back to her people tonight. It was the only explanation. He frowned at the last thought. If it were her own kind, he'd make sure they never did this to anyone again. He'd hunt down every last one of them.

"Get the blanket from behind my seat and lay it out for her," he ordered Vivienne as he cradled Serena in his arms. She immediately jumped into action, laying the blanket out.

"Need me to ride with you?" she begged.

"No." He struggled to get Serena situated on the seat in the least painful position he could think of. "But follow me to my house."

"Okay!" Vivienne agreed and darted to her car.

Jack ran around to the driver's side of his truck and jumped in, firing the engine to life. As he drove, he reached over to brush the hair away from Serena's pale face. She moaned slightly but never opened her eyes.

"I've got you, Serena. Baby, hold on," he whispered as he caressed her cheek. He made a mental checklist of what he needed to do once he got her to his house. He needed to clean her wounds and sew them up. Thank God, he got his paramedic's re-certification this year. It would serve him well tonight...this morning—whatever it was now.

As he rushed down Route 95, he knew he was doing about eighty and Vivienne was struggling to keep up. She was about a quarter of a mile behind him. But as long as she could see him, he'd just keep going because he couldn't slow down. Serena needed help.

Out of nowhere, blue lights appeared behind him.

"Damn!" Jack yelled and slammed his fist on his steering wheel.

What was he going to do now? He forced himself to slow down and pulled off the side of the road on the grassy shoulder. The police cruiser slowed to a stop behind him, lights still on, almost blinding Jack in the process.

Jack watched, detached, as Vivienne drove by at a normal pace. He was glad she kept going, but he'd call her when he got to his house to explain where he lived.

In his rearview mirror, he saw the dark figure exit the police cruiser and start his way. Whispering down to Serena, he pulled the cover almost over her. "*Shhh*, try to be quiet if you can. Okay?"

Serena almost seemed to understand, going still. Jack decided to scoot down in the seat, hoping the police officer wouldn't see the blood on his shirt.

When the officer reached his window, Jack immediately recognized him. The only best friend he had left, Henry Parrish.

"Hey, Henry. Working a late shift?" He wanted to sound as casual as possible, but he knew it was coming out strained and rushed. He only hoped Henry wouldn't want to start a conversation and would let him go.

He smiled from under his Mountie-style hat. "I could ask you the same thing. What's the hurry? I clocked you doing eighty-two. I was worried something was wrong." Suddenly, Henry's face lost its smile, and he leaned in to look at the seat next to Jack.

"Who you got with you?" Henry asked in an almost hushed tone, all business. His demeanor stiffened, and his hand rested on the butt of his gun. He was menacing.

Did he just sniff?

"Hey, relax there, Henry. You look like you could shoot someone."

Henry moved his hand away from his gun and forced a grin. "Oh, sorry. Habit." He shrugged. "So, who's that you got with you?"

"Oh, just a girlfriend of mine who had a little too much to drink. She's fine, just comfortably inebriated." Jack threw in an apologetic smile to make the lie believable.

"A girlfriend, huh?" Henry shined his flashlight into the truck. "I didn't know you had a girlfriend, Jack. You've never mentioned it. In fact, you've never dated anyone that I know of."

Jack stuttered. "Well, she's a girl who is a friend, not a girlfriend."

Why didn't Henry just let him go? He watched his friend's face as he simply stared over at the passenger seat.

"You know I'm sorry about speeding. Honestly, I wasn't paying any attention, and I know that is no excuse, but still. Can't you just cut me some slack, man? I know Mason won't care. Hell, half the people he knows speed," Jack said, hoping to placate Henry.

"*Hmm*," Henry muttered while he continued to look at the seat. Finally, he turned off his flashlight and gave Jack a penetrating glare, the blue of the light dancing off his face. "Is everything okay, Jack?"

Jack bobbed his head a little too earnestly. "Yeah, just tired and wanting to get her home...to her home...not mine. You know what I mean?"

Henry nodded slowly. "And that's it?"

"That's it. Scout's honor." Jack raised his hand with three fingers extended. Was it three fingers or two? He had no idea how a scout saluted.

"Well...okay. Try to drive a little slower next time. I don't want to find your truck wrapped around a tree. It would seriously ruin my night." Henry's voice was strange, almost suspicious. But he was letting him go, which was all Jack wanted.

"Sure. I appreciate this, Henry. I'll call you later." He rolled up his window, as Henry slowly walked back to his car, turning every so often to look back. Henry was acting as weird as Jack was feeling.

Jack made a point of using his turn signal to indicate he was getting back on the road and got to only fifty-five miles per hour until he noticed the lights were off on Henry's cruiser. He didn't see where he eventually went, but he figured he'd turned and went the other direction, because he disappeared from his rearview mirror.

"Close call, baby, but we made it. We made it." Jack stroked Serena's cheek. Serena groaned a little and started breathing shallow, almost like a pant. It made him worry because he knew she could be going into shock.

"Hold on, Serena, hold on." And once again, he sped up.

* * *

In the dim light of his bedroom, Jack was totally exhausted. The sky outside was lightening, so he knew it was almost morning. He sat in a wicker chair in the corner and watched over Serena as she slept.

Serena was quiet and sedated, her wounds stitched and bandaged. She had sustained five long lashes to her back, and for the life of him, he couldn't figure out how that could've happened. People getting whipped went out with the riding of horses as transportation. This just didn't fit with anything he knew.

Right...anything *he* knew.

Vivienne had helped him wash her and get her into some clean clothes. Serena wasn't fully conscious the entire time but mumbled and sometimes thrashed. When they finished tending her, Vivienne collapsed onto his couch, asleep almost before she hit it, but not before threatening his life if he did not wake her at the slightest change in Serena's condition.

What had happened to her and who had hurt her? As soon as she was awake, he was going to get to the bottom of it. He rubbed his eyes, trying to wipe away the fatigue and calm the fury that was building in him. Someone would pay, no doubt about it.

He walked over to his bed, sat down beside her, and reached out to brush her hair back from her face. Sleeping like this, she appeared completely human, with her fangs hidden and her eyes closed. Her skin was porcelain and smooth. He was driven by an innate need to touch her. He knew he was in love with her. Somehow, he was going to figure out how to make it all work, even though it seemed impossible for them to be together.

He thought of the things his mother would say. Like "love conquers all" or "love will find a way." The sayings were all cliché, but suddenly, they seemed like a lifeline for him, a way for him to think they might get to be together. He found himself fingering the necklace she had given him, hoping it was assurance that she wanted the same thing.

He leaned down, kissed her cheek, and then sighed. Upon returning to the chair, he let his eyes close and before he knew it, he was asleep.

Chapter 25: Devon

Morning dawn was breaking through the tree line as Devon emerged from the diner. He stopped and patted his incredibly full belly. He didn't like to eat in the morning, but he decided it might be a good idea today. He was going to be holed up in the local library for as long as it took to ferret out the secrets of this incredibly backward town.

He liked this little diner. The blonde waitress, whose name he learned was Barbara Jean, was cute and quick to fill his coffee cup. He could tell by the way she kept looking over at him that she was attracted to him.

Well now, maybe this town won't be so boring after all.

Walking casually up the sidewalk, he mulled over the conversation with his producer from the night before.

"Any progress?" John Price had demanded.

John had been his producer for the last year. He hadn't been too pleased that the show's ratings were plummeting and that Devon and his crew hadn't found anything salacious or provocative to date. John made it clear before Devon left New York that this had better be something worth pursuing.

Devon attempted to sound confident. "We have some leads. I spoke with the sole survivor of the attack, and it's clear he's hiding something. I've also got the coroner's report, which could be construed as fraud, at least from what I've seen of it."

"Yeah?" John's voice made him seem interested. "When do you think you'll have a draft report to submit?"

Devon scrambled for a response. "I've got some footage of the scene and the police report. I've also talked to some locals—"

"Cut the bullshit and answer the question," John demanded harshly.

"I'll have you something day after tomorrow. It will be rough, but it will be a solid start."

"Good. Keep me posted." He hung up.

Devon fought the same type of schizophrenic tightness he had when he was about to go into a building in Afghanistan to look for insurgents. It was like trying to control his hair-trigger responses, his body tense and ready to shoot to kill. Except now, there were no specific enemies to fetter out, not yet anyway.

He made his way to the library, a neat crimson-bricked two-story building, nicely landscaped with a statue of Benjamin Franklin in the front. A woman sat outside with her small child, looking at a book. The sandy-haired boy glanced up to Devon and smiled. Devon winked back and kept walking.

The smell of books hit him as he opened the doors. It reminded him of his days in high school and its musty old library. It was a sense of déjà vu. Tall rows of neatly stacked books lined each wall. He only needed his third-grade teacher, Ms. Metzger, to approach him to make the trip down memory lane complete.

Devon proceeded toward the info desk, manned by a tiny, gray-haired woman wearing pointy glasses and shuffling from place to place. She was putting books in order on a cart.

"Excuse me, I wonder if you could help me?" Devon tapped his finger on the counter.

Her head lifted, and she eyed him with a tight, uninterested face. Dryly, she replied, "What do you need?"

Devon smiled to loosen her up, which had no effect. "I'm looking for your newspaper archives."

She sighed as if he was bothering her. It wasn't like she was busy, the library was almost empty, and there was no one else at the counter.

"This way," she muttered, and led him between tall shelves of books to a room that housed several microfiche machines, lined up in neat rows back to back.

After giving him a quick tutorial on how to search and print, she finally walked out, seemingly embittered at life.

Devon shook his head, sat down, and got to work.

Chapter 26: **Rahfey**

Rahfey sat sulking in the dark in his small area in the Siege. He was livid, and he couldn't stand any noise or light due to the pressure building in his head.

Serena had walked away from the Siege again, and she was nowhere to be found. When he appeared in Arn's room to tend to her, Arn took great pleasure in telling him she had left during the night.

Fearing she might be bleeding to death, he rushed out of the Siege with two others to hunt for her. They searched for hours, but found her scent abruptly ended at a parking lot. A human had taken her away. Not just any human, *the* human male.

How could she do that to him? Couldn't she see he was doing everything for her own good? Couldn't she see that his beating her was so she would be accepted back into the clan? Otherwise, she would be shunned. He was doing all of this for her own good, yet she kept defying him. It would stop, one way or another. He'd make sure of it. He was tired of being the patient, long-suffering male, waiting for her to wake up and see him there.

Now that she was intended for him, she was basically his mate. Just a few words of assent from her and the ceremony would be complete. Then, he could be with her physically. That aside, he now had control over her until he decided to free her from the Overseers' declaration. But he would never do that. He had waited for years and bid his time until she reached maturity. Once she had, he became a friend to her, patiently trying to be all she needed. When being that close to her was not enough, he'd declared himself to her, and she'd rejected him. He had always thought he could change her mind and sway her to his way of thinking.

He had continued to pursue her willing compliance until he saw her with that human. It was shameful that she'd sullied herself with him.

He shook at the thought of that human touching her. His fist came down so hard on the table where he sat that shadowed items went flying through the air. She was his! No one else would have her, especially not a lowly human.

Rahfey was going to kill that human. Slowly. Painfully. He had escaped the night he and two other humans had camped too close to the Siege. Well, he had to admit they weren't that close. Killing them had been more for fun than anything, but the Overseers didn't need or want to know that.

But still, she had apparently aided the human, and it was a crime punishable by the Reckoning, which few Shilund ever went through or survived. It was a euphemistic term for almost certain death. If he witnessed against Serena, she would be convicted and punished.

As much as he hated what she was doing, he wanted her more. So, he'd keep her secret for now, and one way or another, he was going to finish the job he'd started on the human that night at the camp.

Chapter 27: Jack

Jack woke up to the sound of Serena moving on the bed. Bright light flooded through the window, and the time read one o'clock. Had he actually slept this late? When he moved, he realized he needed to do so slowly as he had been sitting in the chair way too long. Every muscle ached, his joints stiff. He forced himself up and went to the bed.

"Hey. How do you feel?"

Serena's golden eyes regarded him as she lay on her stomach. "I'm feeling a little better. As long as I don't move, I'm okay. Where am I?"

Jack looked around his bedroom that certainly screamed single man and smiled. "I brought you to my house. It seemed like the best place. I hope you don't mind."

"No, I don't mind," she replied softly.

Jack was so captivated by her warm, golden eyes that he didn't know what to say. He reached down and brushed her hair away from her face. He loved how it fanned out over the pillow in soft waves.

"You really scared me," he whispered.

Regret flitted across her face. "I'm sorry. I didn't know Vivienne would call you."

"I'm glad she did. You're safe here; I want you to know that. I won't let anyone hurt you."

Acceptance lit up her expression, and she grinned slightly. Suddenly, she asked, "Where's Vivienne?"

"Right here." Vivienne stood at the door to the bedroom, holding a plate with a sandwich on it in one hand and a cup in the other. "I've been waiting for you to wake up. I'm glad to hear you're feeling better."

Vivienne confidently walked in and sat the items on Jack's dresser. "Jack, I hate to tell you this, but your decorating skills really suck," Vivienne quipped as she stared at him, hands on her hips.

"Hey, now, don't be hatin'. This is my place, and it works for me."

"You must like the prison look." Vivienne shot him an amused look.

Jack smiled at her. She was quick-witted and sharp as a razor's edge. He liked that. After how she had cared for Serena last night, he also knew she cared. Hell, she had even refused to leave.

"So, Rena, you ready to try to eat?" Vivienne's eyes were wary as she waited like an impatient mother.

Serena started to move, and Jack and Vivienne both rushed to her.

"*Whoa*, now, go slow," Jack warned as they helped her to the side of the bed to sit up. Vivienne gently pulled her shirt over her bandaged back.

Serena grimaced but didn't cry out. Jack could tell she appeared to be on the verge of tears. But she squeezed her eyes closed and breathed heavily for a moment before she opened them again.

"Okay?" Vivienne asked worriedly.

Serena opened her eyes and nodded. "Yes, thank you," she replied breathlessly.

Vivienne helped her eat while Jack sat on her other side, watching for any sign she was about ready to pass out or might be in need of something. Serena made it through eating, not uttering a word until she was done.

"I must relieve myself," Serena said with a flushed face. Vivienne immediately helped her stand and led her where she needed to go, explaining how the bathroom worked, and shut the door. Jack watched gratefully as Viv waited against the closed door for her.

Chapter 28: Henry

Henry sat in his cruiser, parked down the street from Jack's house. He'd been here most of the morning, hoping to see Jack head out so he could talk to him. Part of him was a little freaked out at what he felt last night. He couldn't reconcile in his mind what he knew was in the cab of the truck and why Jack was acting like it was all just fine and dandy. Why hadn't Jack just come clean about what was going on? Didn't he trust him enough to tell him?

Henry hands tightened on the steering wheel. Thinking of last night had his past rushing back and hitting him in the head like a two-by-four. It had freaked him out on a level he wasn't even aware he could feel. His chest tightened, and dread floated over him like molten lava. He forced himself to breathe and calm down.

This can't be happening.

When would he ever get away from this and just be able to live his life? When? He hadn't chosen any of this, not his past, not who he was, not any of it. But still, he felt like he was on the edge of a precipice about to fall over into the murky depths.

You idiot, you moved here. If you want to get away from this, you need to get the hell out of Presque Isle.

It was true. If he really wanted to get away from his past, he needed to flee this small town. But there was an anchor keeping him here. Like chains on his soul. Everything kept him from moving forward or going back. He was in purgatory and wished to God someone could pray him out.

He glanced back up to Jack's house. How could Jack be involved? Was he a killer? Was he a savior? Maybe there was another explanation to all of this. His best friend was into something Henry had never imagined. How could he even begin to broach the subject with Jack without revealing too much?

He just needed to bite the bullet and go knock on the door. He started his cruiser and pulled into the long driveway of Jack's house. Taking in a deep breath, he opened his door and stepped out.

In his mind, he played out how he was going to start the conversation. How was he going to get Jack to let his guard down? God, what a mess this was.

Henry reached up and rapped on the door.

Chapter 29: Jack

Jack was in the kitchen, about to head back to the bedroom, when a stern knock sounded on his front door.

He panicked for a moment, wondering who it could be. No one had been over since he had been back. His normal routine of having his firehouse buddies and Henry over on the weekends had long since stopped. He just couldn't bring himself to pretend everything was okay.

Looking down the hall to the bedroom, he could see Vivienne's scared face. He motioned to her it was okay. She nodded and closed the bedroom door.

Jack slowly turned the knob and cracked the front door open a little. There stood Henry Parrish, with a solemn look on his face.

"Hey, Henry." Jack forced a smile, opening the door a bit wider. "What's going on?"

"Mind if I come in?" Henry asked. He seemed as serious as he had last night and that worried Jack a little.

"*Uh*, sure." Jack feigned calm as he threw the door open wide.

Henry walked in and searched around his bare living room. His eyes lingered on the couch, which was made up like a bed.

"Did your company stay last night, Jack?" Henry turned to face him.

"What's going on?" Jack asked as he shut the front door.

"Do you want to tell me what was going on last night?" Henry's unyielding eyes bore into his.

Jack tried to think if he had done anything wrong when Henry had stopped him last night, but he thought he had gotten away clean.

"What do you mean?" Jack leaned against the wall and folded his arms.

Henry sighed heavily and relaxed his stance a little. "Look, Jack, I'm your friend first, a cop second. So, if you are in some trouble or something weird, you can tell me. You know that, right?"

Jack wasn't sure what he was getting at. It was almost like Henry knew something was up, but there was no way he could know. So, Jack just tried to play it cool, even as Henry glanced down his small hallway to the bedroom. Henry seemed to sniff the air again and turned around.

"Look, Henry, I appreciate the stop by and all, but things are fine. I promise you that."

Henry didn't move, just stared at him. "Come on, you can level with me. Whatever it is, I'll help you out, okay? You can trust me. You can *really* trust me."

Jack's anxiety took hold of him, and it was all he could do not to move. He wanted to push Henry right out the door and away from Serena. He wasn't sure what Henry would do if he knew Jack had an unknown species in his bedroom, who hid in the woods and whose clan was responsible for their friends' deaths.

"I think you are taking concern way overboard. What do you think is going on here? Because I'm a little lost at what you're driving at."

Henry sighed and walked around a little. "Jack, I know...I know you didn't have a girl in your truck. I know it was something else."

All the blood drained from his face as they stared at each other. "Henry," Jack began, right as Vivienne came into the living room.

"Jack? Oh!" Vivienne stopped and regarded Henry, smiling broadly. "Well, hello. I didn't know Jack had company. I didn't mean to interrupt." Vivienne fluttered her eyes at Henry and held out her hand. "My name is Vivienne Jam—"

Henry straightened and suddenly returned to cop mode. "Vivienne Jamison, Tom Jamison's daughter. I know who you are, ma'am. Nice to meet you." Henry smiled and shook her hand. Relief washed over Jack that Vivienne had distracted Henry.

"You do?" She shot him a shy, seductive smile. "I'm so glad to meet you. And please don't call me ma'am; you're barely older than I am."

Vivienne pointedly stared down at Henry's left hand, no doubt looking for a wedding band.

"She's the one who was passed out in my truck cab last night," Jack blurted.

Vivienne shot him an angry glare before recognition flashed in her eyes. She nodded, acting embarrassed.

"Yes, well, I was a little drunk, it's true. And if you know my dad, you know he wouldn't take too kindly of me getting that wasted. Jack was a real hero and helped me out of a jam. But, he's not my boyfriend or anything. I'm very single."

Is she about to giggle? Jack would have laughed at that had he not been so worried about Serena in the other room. But Vivienne was batting her lashes and twisting her hands together, almost giddy. God, could this be happening?

Calling EHarmony.

Henry stared dubiously at Jack.

"So, see, Henry, you don't have to be worried. I was just trying to save her from getting a butt chewing from her dad. I let her come here to sleep it off."

Henry eyed Vivienne, who was smiling like she was on TV, and then Jack, who guessed he must look constipated because he was so worried. He knew he was failing at trying to appear relaxed.

"Okay, Jack. Whatever you say, but I meant what I said. I'm here for you, not as a cop, but as a friend."

Before Jack could answer, Vivienne inched closer to Henry. "Do you happen to have a pen?"

Henry appeared confused and then nodded. Like a good Boy Scout, he was prepared and pulled a pen from his pocket.

Vivienne took it with a flourish, lifting up Henry's hand in her own. She started to write on his palm. Surprisingly, Henry allowed it, looking slightly amused.

"Here is my phone number if you want more information, or whatever." She smiled sweetly to him as she finished.

"Thank you, ma'am—I mean, Ms. Jamison...Vivienne," Henry stuttered before composing himself. "I'll be seeing you, Jack. You know where to find me."

Jack opened the door and leaned on it, allowing Henry to move out the door. "Yep, I sure do."

Jack smiled at Henry. Henry wrinkled his nose and then nodded at Vivienne as he ambled out the door.

Jack couldn't get the door closed fast enough and then glared at Vivienne. "What the hell was that? Your phone number? Really?"

"Get the flag pole out of your butt. I like him. I'm single...and he's single." She froze and turned to Jack. "He is still single, right?"

"Not that I should tell you, but yes. He hasn't met anyone since the last time you asked." Jack let out a strong breath. "Do you realize he could have discovered Serena back there? Did you want to try to explain her to him?"

"Relax, Fire Marshall Bill. He didn't have any idea."

"No thanks to you." Jack's temper waned. He was relieved that Henry was gone, and the crisis was over. He didn't know why Henry had stopped by in the first place, but he'd have to be more careful.

"All thanks to me. If I wasn't here, he might have wanted to know who was in your truck last night. So, maybe you should be a little more grateful," she huffed and folded her arms.

He knew she was right. "Sorry," he assented quietly. "Is Serena lying back down?"

Vivienne nodded. "She went to sleep as soon as she hit the bed."

"Good. Are you hungry? You can help yourself to anything in my kitchen."

"No, thanks. I'm going to go home, have a shower, and try to convince my folks I just left really early this morning before they got up to go to the gym or something." She sighed, picked up her purse, and moved closer to the door.

"Come on, aren't you eighteen? Can't you come and go as you please?" Jack smirked.

"Nineteen," she corrected. "And if you knew my folks, you'd know it's the old 'their house, their rules' type of thing. They're cool mostly. They just want to know if I'm gone and when I'm coming home. I didn't exactly tell them I was leaving in the middle of the night."

Jack nodded and she headed for the door.

"Call me if Serena has any change or you need me. I'll be back later," she called over her shoulder.

"Will do."

Vivienne paused at the door. "Oh, when do you go to work?"

Jack frowned. Work. He had totally forgotten. He was to go in tonight, and it was his first day doing full duty. He couldn't call in his first day back, but he couldn't very well leave Serena on her own, not as hurt as she was.

"I'm supposed to work tonight, but I don't want to leave Serena here alone."

Vivienne raised her hands. "No worries, I'll head over after my shift is done and stay with her. I only work four hours tonight."

Serena had a great friend in Vivienne. He found himself smiling at her. "That would be great, thank you."

She grinned. "It's what I do. You got my number if you need me in the meantime. Later, gator." Vivienne breezed out the door, leaving Jack alone in his living room.

Chapter 30: **Devon**

Devon, freshly shaven and wearing his best cammies, gazed unflinchingly into the eye of the camera. He stood at the campsite where the firefighters had been attacked and died. The light was fading and it gave the forest a spooky vibe, definitely something to take advantage of.

"It happened here, among the tall oaks and bushy pine trees, late one summer evening in the Aroostook National Forest outside of Presque Isle, Maine. Three men looking for a fun weekend camping got more than they bargained for. It was a collision course with disaster. Their innocent decision to stay at this very site would cost two of them their lives, the other barely making it out with his. They discovered too late that the woods were inhabited by brutal creatures that have been rumored to reside in this forest for hundreds of years, killing indiscriminately and completely unstoppable. All this and more on the next episode of *Fringe Hunters*."

Tom yelled, "Cut! I think that will be enough for now."

Devon relaxed. "Yeah, I do too. I sent my draft dialogue to Price, so I hope it's enough to get him off my back." He was under John Price's thumb in a big way. He couldn't do anything without him wanting the "who, what, when, where, why, and how" of everything he did. He could appreciate his diligence in being a producer, but he needed to relax just a hair.

Tom nodded as he broke down the camera and tripod to put in a case that lay beside his feet.

"You ready to start the trek to put out the cameras?" Tom eyed Devon, waiting for a reply.

Boy, was he ever. Those cameras were going to be the thing that really saved this story. Devon could tell people about it all he wanted, but to see the creatures in living color would blow this whole thing out of the water.

Devon thought about the failed attempt at getting footage of a Bigfoot in California a few months ago. But this situation was different. He had the coroner's report and there was no way a cougar had killed those two men. No, something more menacing was at work.

Devon searched the area again. "Yeah, I think so. We've got

six, right?" Devon finally turned to Tom.

"Yep, and they should have about twenty-four hours of storage. So, that should give us plenty of time to hook up to the transmitters and download it from the room. I love technology." Tom smiled, displaying his crooked teeth.

"Good deal."

Devon knew there was something out there, something not human, and he was going to crack this secret wide open. All the obscure tales he'd located in the library from over the years spun together a highly interesting story. There was something like a man out here, with cat-like eyes and fangs. No one ever got a good photo of it, but different people throughout the years had seen it. And Devon was going to be the one to document it and become famous. And hopefully, that would allow his past to finally die once and for all in his head.

"Let's get going. We have a lot of ground to cover in a short amount of time." Tom slung the camera case onto his back and began to hike, Devon close on his heels.

Chapter 31: **Serena**

Serena was lying on her stomach with her hands under her cheek, staring out the window with minimal interest as the daylight faded into night.

She could think clearer and her body ached only slightly. But the best part? She lay on Jack's bed, his scent all over the sheets and everything in the room. He surrounded her—invading her almost. It was a welcomed feeling. She closed her eyes and breathed in deep. How she loved this dark-haired human. A small voice reminded her their time was short and she should revel in each moment that they had together.

She got up on her hands and knees, and eased herself down into a sitting position beside the bed. Her back was much better and would be completely healed in a day or two. Thinking about having to leave that soon made her heart stop. She didn't want to go back and face Rahfey, the Overseers, and all the stuff that was hanging out there. No, she wanted to stay right here, safe with Jack.

It wasn't possible, she knew. But that didn't stop her from wishing it was. Every ounce of her wanted Jack. For her, there could be no other. But she could never be with him, so she'd accept what little bit of happiness they could have in the few moments they shared. Then she'd have to figure out how to say goodbye.

As she stood to gently put on her shirt, she gazed around the room, and a photograph on the dresser caught her attention. In it, Jack appeared to be about twelve with what were probably his mother and father. She was struck how much of a mix of his parents Jack was. A small, blonde girl, no older than six, stood beside him. Her square, pearly teeth shone from between her ruby-red lips. Her cheeks were a little flushed like she had been running. This must be Jack's sister, the one who died when she was little.

A pang of sorrow shot through her. It must be horrible to lose a sibling. When Jack spoke of Lilly during one of their phone conversations, he spoke mournfully and at times, she could almost hear a hint of guilt. She knew he missed her greatly, and the pain of loss seemed raw and unhealed, almost like it had just happened. His wound was a festering mess. He had rushed past the discussion to the next subject, so she didn't pursue it any more.

Serena wondered what it would be like if she lost Arn. Would she be like Jack, forever locked in loss? It made her shudder to think of Arn no longer being there. He was the only family she'd ever had. Her parents were but flashes of memory in her head. A big unknown. Arn never brought them up, but if she had questions, he'd respond with succinct answers that revealed little. Someday, she hoped she learned more about them and how they'd died. All she had now were names, Sisika and Nathan, but knew nothing much about who they had been.

She walked over to a chest of drawers and saw various items on the top. A small bowl in the shape of a shell held various coins of human money. She picked some up and examined it curiously. Putting it back down, she saw a small plastic card with a picture of Jack on it.

Lifting it up, she read it. "Jackson Ty Day, PFF, Presque Isle Fire Division." Jack's photo was a stern looking image. She took her fingertips and trailed along his buzz cut and smiled. His hair was longer now and she found she preferred it that way than to this image. She held the card for a moment, but found herself placing it in her pocket. Hopefully he wouldn't miss it.

A soft tap on the door pulled her out of her musings. Jack slowly stuck his head in. She gently lowered her hands and turned toward him, hoping that he hadn't seen what she had just done.

"Serena?" He glanced to the bed and then over to her. "What are you doing up?" His whole body was through the door in a matter of seconds. He put his hands under her arm as if to steady her.

"Let's get you back to bed." Jack tried to lead her to it, but Serena protested.

"No, I'm okay. Really, Jack, I'm much better."

Jack's brow furrowed. "I hate to disagree with you, but you have some nasty wounds on your back. Those are going to take a while to heal, and the only way they are going to do that is if you lie down and rest."

Serena smiled. "Look at my back." She allowed him to lift her shirt, and he did so gently and gasped.

"How in the world...?"

"My kind heals quickly," she replied with a shrug.

His fingertips lightly traced down the furrows in her back, causing her to shudder.

"It looks like the stitches are able to be taken out. That's amazing."

She tried not to think too much about him touching her so

intimately. She knew it was clinical, but part of her wanted it to mean more. Maybe he loved her, too. As much as she wanted to believe that, the doubtful side of her said otherwise. The unwelcomed memory of him screaming 'What are you?' came rushing back to her. She remembered the fear and loathing on his face. Even though she didn't see him looking at her that way now, she still wondered if those feelings were still there in him somewhere.

Jack lowered her shirt, turning her around. He rubbed her arms and then pulled her to him. His lips came down on her head, and he sighed in relief.

"I'm so glad you're getting better. I couldn't stand how badly you were hurt."

She could hear his heart beating and smelled a mixture of soap and the fragrance that was all him. She'd been breathing him in all day. It was intoxicating and heady. She held him close to her and sighed contentedly, his arms enclosing her like protection and safety.

Raising her eyes to gaze into his blazing stare, she began, "I..."

Before she could finish, his lips found hers, possessing her, adoring her. His hands tugged her closer as the kiss deepened, and every part of her came alive. Her stomach fluttered and rolled with an excitement she had never known before. She couldn't think because his kiss was making her muddled and incoherent. The only things she knew for sure were she didn't want him to stop and she wanted him closer to her.

A purr built in the back of her throat from the pleasure flooding her. Its rhythmic vibration filled the room, but she couldn't stop. Her mind and senses were filled up with Jack, and only Jack. And for the first time in her life, she wanted to bare all she was to a male.

Jack pulled back, panting, trying to catch his breath. But he didn't let her go. His blue eyes glowed, and they searched hers. "Are you okay?"

"I was a moment ago before you pulled away." Serena smiled. "You...didn't have to stop."

A sheepish grin appeared on Jack's face. "I didn't want to, believe me, but it's probably better for you that I do. Plus, I have to be at work in twenty minutes." He trailed his fingers down her face.

"I like how you kiss and hold me," Serena confessed, but he was probably right they should stop. There was a struggle between her desperate need and uncontrollable want of him.

"You are so beautiful. So entirely breathtaking and desirable. I can't believe I am standing here with you in my arms. It's too good to be true."

The words warmed her more than his touch. She lowered her eyes from his. "I want you to know..." Dare she say it? "I believe I am what the humans call...in love with you."

She stared at the yellow logo on the chest of his blue shirt, afraid to look up into his face, fearful of seeing rejection, sympathy, or even regret. No, she didn't want to see it, and as much as she wanted him to return her feelings, she had accepted that he couldn't or wouldn't love her back.

"Oh Serena, I—" Jack began, but Serena turned from him.

"I know you are human, and I'm Shilund, and I don't ask for you to return my feelings—"

Jack drew her back to him and tilted her head up so that she had no choice but to look at him. She felt so exposed to him that she closed her eyes. She didn't want to see his face.

"Serena, look at me."

She waited for a few moments before slowly opening her eyes.

His face was glowing. He leaned in, kissed her softly, and pulled back. "I'm in love with you, too," he breathed against her skin. "You make me feel alive again." His lips found hers, giving her another hungry kiss.

As much as Serena wanted to give in, she pulled back and away from his hold. His eyes crinkled in confusion.

"But we cannot be together," she protested. "I know this. You know this." She searched around the room for some sort of answer, anything, to help her find a resolution.

"Why not? Why can't we be together?" Jack gripped her arm. "There is nothing that can keep us apart."

"Except our worlds." She met his eyes head on. "We are different in all ways. How could we be together?"

"Just like we are, right here and now. We are not as different as you think. And although it will be a challenge, I'm willing to take it on. Hell, I'd take on anything, just to have you in my life." His eyes were begging, and Serena wanted to drown in them, forget their irreconcilable lives, and just be in this moment. But the reality was it wasn't that easy.

"We can't. I live in the Shilund world and you live in the human world. How can we do this?" Truth be told, she wasn't sure where she would even go when she finished healing. She needed to consider she was an outcast and would have to live as a nomad.

"How can we not?" he countered. "Do you love me?"

"It's impossible." Tears formed in her eyes, and she fought to hold them off. She didn't want to appear weak to him.

"Do. You. Love. Me?" he demanded.

"Yes, with everything I am," she whispered.

He pulled her close to him, and she willingly went into his arms.

"Then we will find a way, I promise. Please don't give up on us. Please."

He pressed a soft kiss on the top of her head. Her insides ached for this, to give in and accept it as a possibility. How she wanted him. She never wanted to be parted from him.

"Okay, Jack. Okay. We'll find a way."

She closed her eyes tight and just held him. This human loved her. Her heart wanted to sing and dance, but her doubts told her this was foolish, and this would be taken from her somehow.

Jack leaned back and rubbed her arms, smiling reassuringly. "I hate to go, but I have to work tonight. Vivienne should be over any moment now. She's going to stay the night. So you guys have the run of my house. No wild parties, okay? I don't want to find my toilet out on the lawn." Jack laughed.

Serena's eyebrows rose in a question.

Jack smiled. "Never mind, it happened once to Chris..." Pain was etched deep on his face and he sucked in a deep breath. "Anyway, you and Vivienne just relax here, and help yourself to anything in my kitchen."

Serena loved the thought of being here, surrounded by his things, being a part of his life, and getting to share that with Vivienne. "It will be good to see her."

Jack reached into his closet and grabbed a bag. "I'll be back in the morning. Luckily, I don't have to pull a three-day shift. My boss is letting me ease into full duty." He grinned again. "Just stay here and rest, okay?"

Serena nodded, just as he leaned in and kissed her again. He made his way out of the house and then she heard his truck leaving the garage. She sat down, feeling like she must be glowing because she was so blissful. He loved her, and she loved him. For once in her life, she was truly happy.

Chapter 32: **Rahfey**

Rahfey loved how the cool night surrounded him. He inhaled a lungful, his senses heightening. Tonight, he was going to be the hunter, and he couldn't wait to get his prey.

He had never had anyone challenge him like this, especially a female. A male of any type of honor would take steps to protect his female against any who would try to abscond with her virtue. Add in that it was a human, and Rahfey knew what needed to be done to protect her as his future mate.

He made quick time of running to an abandoned barn on Conant Road, five miles out of town. It stood alone, the humans no longer using it for any type of commerce. The woods and brush choked it, and the entrance to the barn had almost completely grown over.

It was a perfect place to hatch his plan and set his trap. He walked around the structure methodically, gazing up to the second story, imagining how this would play out. He grinned while his fingers trailed along the rough, weathered wood. It couldn't come quick enough for him.

He walked around to the backside of the barn and pushed in the door, which protested with a loud creak and opened inward with a trail of cobwebs. Stepping in, he stared at the dried hay and ancient wood. No one had been in this barn in years; it was an old, abandoned relic from the humans.

His eyes tracked the movement of mice as they raced along the walls, fearful of the invader to their home. The smell of musky wood and dirt filled his nose, getting decidedly stronger as he started scraping his feet against the ground, making a circle in the middle of the floor. After pushing back all the debris he could, he lined stacks of loose twigs along the walls of the barn.

Once he was satisfied with the pile, he stepped back and pulled a piece of flint from his pants. He struck the flint against the kindling and it immediately roared into a fire.

Rahfey grinned and ran from the premises to await the arrival of his victim. Soon, very soon, he would eliminate the last obstacle to getting that which was rightfully his.

Chapter 33: **Jack**

It was a quiet night at the firehouse, and Jack was glad. The firehouse had been cleaned inside and out, everyone pitching in over the past few days. Now some of the men were up in the lounge watching TV. He wasn't much interested in that, so he stood outside, gazing up at the stars shining down on him.

Every part of him was alive for once in his life. He knew this was due to the beautiful girl back at his house. His love for her was a total surprise. He had almost given up that he'd meet anyone. Presque Isle was such a small town, and he knew every eligible female there was. The chance he'd find someone was slim to none, and Presque Isle was the largest city in Aroostook County. So, he'd given up the notion of a romantic relationship.

Serena had come into his life like a shooting star against a black sky, blazing furious light in his darkness. She awoke something in him he had never felt, not even in his high school crushes. Warmth radiated through him, and he couldn't wait to get back to her. He wondered how she was. He knew Vivienne wouldn't hesitate to call him if she needed to. But still, he wanted to be there with her.

Crossing his arms, he smiled at the realization that Serena loved him, too. They would figure this all out. However hard it would be, no matter the obstacle, they would be together. Somehow.

A blaring set of tones sounded through the firehouse, interrupting the quiet of the evening. A fire had been called in. Jack rushed to his boots and trousers, jumping in and snapping the boots shut and the suspenders over his shoulders.

A disembodied female voice called out, "Unit 900, Unit 900, report of a fully involved barn fire at 1036 Conant Road. Repeating Unit 900, Unit 900, report of a fully involved barn fire at 1036 Conant Road."

Jack pulled on his coat, gloves, hood, and helmet and dashed onto the engine as its lights came on.

Chief Merchant responded, "10-4, Engines 908 and 909 in route to the scene, Code 3."

The female voice reverberated throughout. "Copy, 23:46"

All the men were on the truck in a matter of seconds. The

lights were on, and the siren began to wail as they tore out of the firehouse.

Adrenaline coursed through his veins as they raced through the town and out to the country road. Even though he had been on many other calls before, each one affected him the same. You never knew what the outcome would be, and you needed to remain completely focused so you or someone you loved didn't get killed.

It didn't take long before the engine pulled up to the blazing barn. Immediately behind them, another engine arrived. The barn was a glowing gold and auburn that jerked in a macabre dance against the obscure night. The cracks and pops were loud as the fire ate through the wood. No part of the barn was left untouched by the flames.

The truck got into position so that the crew could pull off the hose and start draining the engines of their reserve in order to put out the inferno.

The heat was intense and scorched Jack's face. Working alongside Mac Bray, he wrestled the hose to the back of the barn to douse it with the strong spray. The thicket was dense and hard to walk through, but with great effort, he and his partner succeeded in making it to the back. Mac opened the nozzle and began to sweep against the blaze.

The water seemed to make no difference at first, appearing only to anger the fire, but after a few minutes, it started to recede. However, at this rate, the engines would be sucked dry and they'd have to draft from a nearby pond or other water source. He only hoped the water supply they had would be enough. In the end, they might have to consider the barn a complete loss and take measures to only contain the fire and keep it from jumping to the thick, surrounding brush.

"I need to move. Can you get me some slack?" Mac yelled above the noise.

"On it!" Jack replied.

Moving back to pull on more hose, he saw how it snaked almost hidden through the high grass along the side of the barn. Pulling as hard as he could to get slack so Mac would have an easier time of it, he found the hose wouldn't give. Figuring it must be caught on something, he followed its path to see what it was wrapped around.

Suddenly, his feet left the ground, and he landed on his back in a bone-crushing thud. Something had the back of his collar, and he was quickly being pulled deeper into the woods. Trying to stop his movement by grabbing onto something, he only succeeded in clawing dirt. His movement continued unabated.

He yelled, but no one heard him above the shouts of the other firemen and the sound of the blaze. What was pulling him? He struggled again against the force that was dragging him along, but it was strong, much stronger than he was. Just before he lost consciousness, he saw the face he'd never wanted to see again. A hand came down and it went black.

Chapter 34: Henry

Henry heard the fire call over his radio as he stood chatting with Barbara Jean after he picked up some coffee before the diner closed.

After nodding to her, he rushed to his cruiser to head out to Conant Road. The night had been quiet, and this was a nice diversion. He always liked to see the firefighters put out the fires, moving around the blaze like dancers at a waltz. It was awesome to see them at work. He admired what they did. They were the type of heroes that worked quietly, saving homes and lives and never asking for any type of thanks.

It occurred to him that he might see Jack there. He was back on reduced duty so chances were good. He frowned, knowing he would have to get answers from him sooner or later. Why didn't Jack want to admit he was involved in something unbelievable? Henry wasn't going to give up.

Pulling up to the fire, he could see the firefighters rushing around to get the blaze under control. They were attacking it from all sides. It was profoundly loud, a mixture of yelling and crackling wood. Ghoulish shadows swayed on the perimeter around the blaze, making it look like demons dancing around a bonfire. The blaze appeared to be surrendering to the efforts of the men scurrying around it, dousing it with water.

Henry searched the names written on the backs of the firefighters and realized he didn't see Jack anywhere.

Henry found Bob Merchant, who stood with his arms folded, his large helmet shadowing his eyes.

"Nice bonfire you got here. If you wanted to roast marshmallows, you should have told me. I would have brought my fire pit to the firehouse. No need for all this drama." Henry snorted.

Bob furrowed his eyebrows and smiled, shaking his head as he turned back to supervise the efforts. "Yeah, well, who wants the cops involved when the firemen can do it better?"

Henry chuckled. "Is Jack working tonight?" he asked, while still checking around.

"Yeah, he's right over there..." A look of confusion crossed Bob's face. "Well, he was over there, backing up Mac."

Henry saw Brad Likins managing the hose with Mac Bray, but

no sign of Jack.

The chief headed over to the side of the barn where Brad and Mac were.

"Say, where is Day?" Bob demanded.

Mac struggled to hold onto the hose while Brad backed him up.

"He said he was going to get me more slack, and that was the last I saw him. Brad came over and took his place."

The chief frowned, very perplexed. "Likins, did you see Day?"

Brad Likins shook his head. "No, sir, I saw Bray struggling here, so I came over to help with the hose."

The chief was immediately on his radio. "Unit 1 to Day. Come in, Day."

Only static came from the radio. Chief Merchant put the radio up to his lips again. "Unit 1 to all crew. Please account for each man and advise if anyone is with Jack Day."

That was when Henry smelled it. It wafted on the wind from the woods like a lightning bolt. He inhaled, and his defenses went on high alert.

He wandered toward the smell while Chief Merchant continued to try to locate Jack over the radio. But all of the replies were that no one knew where he was.

Henry inhaled again and followed the scent out into the woods, trying not to draw attention. Jack's scent was mixed with something else...a Shilund, from the smell of it, and it smelled fresh. And it was not the same one he'd encountered in Jack's truck or his home. Whatever the reason for Jack's scent to be mixed with it here couldn't be good. He knew Jack well enough to know that he wouldn't just walk off a call, which meant he was taken.

He needed to follow the scent and find out what happened. If a Shilund had him, they would be long gone and into places in the forest he was unfamiliar with. But where would a Shilund take a human? He had no idea, but it occurred to him that someone else might.

Running toward his cruiser, he knew of only one place he might find out who it was and why they wanted Jack. He had to get to Jack's house.

Bob Merchant stared at him in question.

"Call!" Henry said by way of explanation, jumped into his cruiser, and sped off down the road.

Chapter 35: **Serena**

"And you watch this for entertainment?" Serena asked Vivienne as they both sat sprawled on Jack's couch watching TV and eating popcorn. Serena realized she liked popcorn with its sweet, oily crunch.

"Yeah, it is. I mean, not all of it is good, but there are some good shows—*NCIS*, anything on Animal Planet, and of course, *Hoarders*. That show makes me feel like my room is immaculate, no matter what my mom says."

"*Hoarders*?" Serena asked.

As Vivienne explained, Serena couldn't understand why a show about people who kept things would be something to watch. She'd never understand humans.

Vivienne opened her mouth to say something as a car screeched its tires to a stop in Jack's driveway.

"Get to the bedroom, now!" Vivienne commanded, and Serena rushed back and shut the door. Her heart pounded as loudly as the banging on Jack's front door. The walls vibrated as the door flung open.

A loud, male voice asked, "Where are they?"

"Where is who?" Vivienne answered with a smooth innocence.

"Are they in the back?" he demanded. Serena could tell the voice was getting louder, which meant he was coming closer to the bedroom.

Vivienne protested, "I don't care if you are a hot-looking cop; you can't just barge in here and go back there. Stop! I mean it!"

"I don't have time for this!" the man, now angry, argued, and the door flew open as Serena backed up.

Serena couldn't decide if she should bolt out the window, which would probably hurt, or if she should stay and face this menace. As she was deciding she caught his scent and was immediately confused. He appeared human, but his smell suggested otherwise.

A blond man wearing a policeman's uniform approached her, stopping when she raised her hands.

"Look, I don't know who you are or why you are here, but Jack's in trouble. I need your help," the policeman said, looking at Serena.

"Jack is in trouble?" Her heart fluttered wildly. She was stuck between wanting to run from the man and wanting to rush to him to demand answers. Pressing her back against the wall, she studied him. "What are you? You look human, but you are not. I can tell from your scent." Serena was afraid this was all a ruse to lure her from Jack's, but she didn't think the Shilunds in her clan would go to these lengths.

The blond man gazed at her for a moment before removing his wallet and pulling out an insignia. Walking closer to Serena, he offered it to her.

"Don't you touch her!" Vivienne shouted as she rushed forward and jerked hard on the man's arm.

"It's okay, Vivienne," Serena said as she took the Insignia from his hand. Staring at it, she glanced up to the man. "Why are you not with your clan?"

"What? Clan?" Vivienne demanded as she searched between the two of them. "What the hell is going on?"

The man sighed loudly. "They are out west, in Arizona. They shunned me when I was a child."

Serena looked at the insignia and recognized the lineage in a portion of it, but she didn't want to get into that now. She held it up for him to take back and he did so, putting it back in his wallet.

"Only your mother's clan is out west," she replied quietly. "How is it you look human?"

The man studied her for a moment, then reached up to his eye and removed a contact. Staring at her was a Shilund eye, a beautiful green eye with a cat-like iris. "My name is Henry Parrish. I've lived as a human for nineteen years." Henry popped the lens back in and then leveled his gaze at Serena. "Please, I'll explain later. I need your help. Jack is in trouble."

"He's one of you?" Vivienne whispered, disbelief etched on her face.

"What has happened to Jack?" she demanded, ignoring Vivienne's question for now.

"A Shilund has taken him. I smelled their scent. Apparently, they pulled him into the woods when he was on a call. I can only guess they took him to their Siege. I don't know where it is, but I venture that you do."

"Yes, I do! There is no time to waste; we must go now!" Serena rushed to Henry as he moved in agreement toward the door.

"Stay here, Vivienne," Serena ordered when she started to follow.

"No! Serena, I can help!" Vivienne protested.

Henry immediately turned to Vivienne, leaning slightly into her. "Please, beautiful, stay here. You'll be safer. Please."

Vivienne seemed mesmerized for a moment, then crossed her arms and acquiesced. "Fine, Hank." She pouted. "But you owe me a phone call and date after this."

A tiny smile crept across Henry's face. "It's a deal." He caressed her arm and then bolted out the door.

Was there something going on between this human impostor and Vivienne? Why hadn't she told her? Serena made a point to ask her about this later.

She turned to Vivienne and hugged her. "I will be back."

"You better." Vivienne's eyes widened and she chewed on her lip. Serena squeezed her arms and then rushed out after Henry.

Henry got into the car. She studied the handle and after a couple of tries, figured out how to open it. She sat down in the boxy vehicle. The small space had her heart thudding and her chest tightening. She tried to take it all in.

"You act like you've never been in a car before," Henry said.

"Well, I rode in Jack's truck, but I was...well...injured. So this would be the first time I'm aware of it." She watched Henry put a strap over his body and lock it into place.

"Seatbelt," he demanded and pointed to her side. She mimicked his actions and put the shiny metallic end of the strap into a square snap. When it clicked in place, how it restrained her made her uncomfortable.

Henry pulled down on a stick and the vehicle moved. It was odd to feel yourself moving without making any effort at all. It reminded her of floating in the lake.

"So, where to?" Henry asked as he turned a circular wheel that seemed to direct the car's movements. She had seen plenty of cars, but didn't really understand much how they worked. It was fascinating.

"Head toward the Aroostook National Forest," she said and Henry nodded and began driving very fast.

"Hold on."

Serena tried to comply, but wasn't sure what she could hold on to that would make her feel any less like she were being hurled off a cliff. She closed her eyes and just thought about Jack and hoped he was okay.

Chapter 36: Jack

Jack was being dragged through the forest by the scruff of the neck, and wasn't it déjà vu? Except now, instead of a nice, padded travois of tree leaves his fire coat was his only protection. Plus, his hands and feet were bound, so it wasn't very comfortable.

He recalled right before he blacked out, or was knocked out, the hideous face of that other Shilund he'd seen at Serena's cabin. What was his name? Jack struggled to remember, and then it came to him. Rahfey, which was the name Serena used. But why was this Rahfey dragging him along?

Jack struggled to see in front of him. "Rahfey? What are you doing? Let me go."

Suddenly, he was dropped to the ground, and Rahfey was in his face. "Do not speak to me, human! You are condemned to die, and unless you want me to kill you here and now, you will be silent!" Rahfey backhanded Jack. He immediately tasted blood and spit it out.

"Untie me right now! You want to settle this like men then I'm more than ready to get down to it!" The heat rose up in his face like a storm and he wanted to kick this Rahfey's ass. Now that he was healthy, he could probably do some damage to him.

Another punch landed on his face. "Silence!

Irritable, Jack spit again and growled, "Coward! Untie me and try that again! I guarantee you it won't be that easy!"

Rahfey swung to hit Jack again, but Jack blocked his hand with his arms, grabbed a hold of his collar, and began to choke Rahfey. Jack was no match for him, and his hand was pulled away as easily as an adult to a child.

"I will enjoy cutting out your heart, the same way I did your two friends. They died painfully slow deaths, and I rather enjoyed watching them bleed out," Rahfey sneered.

Jack's heart pounded hard, and his vision went wonky. His temper was lit. He wanted to rip this Shilund apart, limb-by-limb.

I am going to kill you. One way or another, I am going to kill you.

"Why wait? Untie me if you think you are man enough to do it. Let's settle this right here and now. I'm not afraid of you." Jack struggled against his bonds.

Rahfey smiled. "As much as I'd like to do that, we need to do this a little more publicly. You need to be an example and a warning to Serena." Rahfey leaned into Jack and sniffed. "I can smell her all over you." He leaned back and glared at Jack. "I will have to make sure I get your human stench off of her. I will try to make it enjoyable for her so she will never think of you again, you filthy human."

"You stay away from her, you hear me? Touch her and I will kill you. I promise you that," Jack shouted.

Rahfey struck him again, hard against the side of his head. "Oh, you'll get your chance to fight me. Don't you worry. Although, you'll be the one who will die, not me."

"What is it that eats at you Rahfey? The fact that she doesn't want you or that she has picked me? A lowly human, by your standards. She can probably see right through you and doesn't want you. Let me clue you in on a little secret, she'll never want you. Do you hear me?"

"Shut up!" Rahfey screamed as he struck Jack hard in the face again.

Jack glared up at him. "A little too close to the truth? You are pathetic!" Jack spat in Rahfey's face and the spittle ran down his cheek.

Blood rushed up into Rahfey's cheeks and with that, Rahfey kicked Jack in the face, effectively ending the conversation.

Chapter 37: **Serena**

Serena hated that she was walking down the hidden trail she planned to never see again. The foliage surrounding it seemed to smother her. When she had left nights ago, her intention was to never return. She figured she'd be a nomad and live alone close to Jack. That was the loose plan. Now, here she stood, right back on familiar ground with Henry trailing behind her.

She kept turning over in her mind how Henry was living in the human world, living among them and looking like them. Of course, she had known immediately that he was a Shilund; it was his scent. But, he appeared human. His teeth were normal, and she knew now his eyes had contacts—imposter in the human world.

Even more troubling was the lineage in his insignia. That was shocking. She idly wondered if Henry knew about where he came from and who he really was.

She had a million questions, but for now, they would have to wait. They needed to find Jack first. He was the priority. She suspected she knew who had taken him. But she wasn't entirely sure. They would regret it if they hurt him, and she only prayed they would reach Jack before anything drastic occurred.

Pushing through the heavy brush, Serena questioned, "Do you have a Shilund name, or do you prefer the human one you use?"

Serena kept moving forward, Henry trailing behind her. She'd almost given up that he would reply, but then, he spoke.

"Leif was my name."

Serena nodded her head. "Which do you prefer?"

"Well, I haven't been called Leif since I was a child, so I suppose Henry is fine. If you called me Leif, I might not answer." A smile was in his voice.

"Henry it is. You know that what we are walking into is highly likely to be violent, right? If the one I suspect has taken him, he'll kill Jack to punish me before the Overseers. He'll stop at nothing. He hates humans."

"I recognized his scent around the crime scene where Adam Hensley and Chris Jenkins were killed. So, I figured his motives weren't to sit down and have a beer with him."

So, that narrowed it down for Serena. It was either Rahfey or some of his underlings. This was such a mess. Why couldn't Rahfey just leave her alone? There were so many other females in the Siege willing to be his mate. She sighed and kept her feet moving at a human pace. Even though she knew Henry was a Shilund, she wasn't sure of his abilities and didn't want to outrun him.

As they neared the area where they would be seen by the sentinels on watch, she stopped and turned to Henry, who now wore only a white T-shirt and his uniform pants. She knew he had a gun at the small of his back and at his ankle. He had made sure that she knew he was armed. He waited and watched her, his body tight.

"When we get there, you must let me speak, okay? They will not listen to you, as you appear to have aligned yourself with humans and will look as a traitor to your own kind. Your lineage may not even protect you. Do you understand?"

"My lineage?" Henry replied, confused.

"Do you understand?" she pushed.

Henry nodded. Reaching up, he removed his contacts to show his Shilund eyes, tossing them aside. Serena watched every move of his hands and then he grinned slightly, blinking those familiar, Shilund green eyes.

"I do."

"All right, we are getting ready to approach the outer rim of the Siege. We have guards who are under orders to kill any strangers that dare enter. I just hope that they let me explain you before they strike you down. The mere fact you are Shilund will probably give them pause."

Trouble ran across Henry's face and then he nodded once, rolling his shoulders as if preparing for a battle. And then he was downright composed.

"Have your insignia handy," she demanded.

Henry patted his pocket. "It's within reach." He grinned. "Now let's go kick some ass."

Serena wanted to smile, she truly did. But she was worried about Jack and what was happening to him. Thankfully, Henry seemed ready. He was utterly calm.

Turning, she continued forward on the path until she knew they were in eyesight of the guards. Standing by the creek, she announced loudly, "Do not harm the Shilund with me. His father is of our clan and he has a right to be here."

She waited, watched, and spotted the Shilund sentinels in the trees. Human eyes could not see them, but she could see as well in the dark as in the light. No one moved, so Serena walked up the hill to the cave entrance.

"Come on," she whispered, looking around. She was feeling like maybe this wouldn't be so bad. After all, they had made it without issue. It wasn't until she reached out to remove the vines concealing the opening that the sentinels descended upon them like hawks reaching their prey.

The first two took a hold of Henry and one grabbed her. She struggled against the urge to gouge out the eyes of the one who held her, but she needed to stay calm. Henry was clenching his jaw but not fighting the guards. One of them made a show of removing his gun from his back.

"Someone's been looking for you," one of the males said to her with an air of disgust.

"Well, here I am, looks like you found me," she said sharply. No doubt Rahfey had been going crazy wondering where she had been.

"Show your insignia!" the one who held her bellowed to Henry.

"If they would let me go, I would," Henry complained through clenched teeth. His face was red, and he tried not to struggle, controlling the power that seemed to radiate off him.

The one holding Serena made a noise of assent, and Henry was released. He jerked away in irritation.

"You move carefully now," the dark-haired one that had held him warned.

Henry held his hands out to show he was not going to move fast or do anything stupid. He slowly reached into his pocket and then presented his insignia. The dark-haired one swore and backed away with his partner.

Take that, you jerks!

Serena found herself smiling as the rough hands released her. Confusion marred Henry's face as he watched the two retreat after returning his gun. The one who had held Serena made a motion for them to enter the Siege and disappeared with his partners.

When they were hidden again in the trees, Henry turned the insignia over in his hands and then tilted his head toward her. "What was that all about?"

You have no idea, do you? "You are just scary, is all." She bit back a giggle.

Serena knew he'd get this reaction everywhere in the Siege. She just wondered if anyone would tell him why. Should she let him in on it before they went inside? No, there wasn't time. Jack could be hurt or worse. Serena didn't want to consider the worse.

She moved the vines out of her way, revealing the opening, and she and Henry quickly moved inside. Upon seeing the main cavern that was their communal gathering place below, she involuntarily shivered. The last time she was there, she was whipped into unconsciousness. Well, she would be strong and face this down, anything for Jack.

She wasn't sure if she should be concerned that Jack was not displayed here to be an example before the clan. She made her way down into the cave and could sense Henry following.

Along the periphery were various Shilund going about their daily meanderings, until they saw Serena and Henry. A few scurried away, while some stopped and stared.

Yes, go tell Rahfey and the Overseers we are here! Do it quickly, she thought with disgust, watching some run away.

She knew right where she should go and made her way down a stone corridor to her and Arn's quarters. Pulling the cloth door back, she saw Arn reading. His head lifted, and he yelled.

"Serena! Oh, thank God!" Her father came to her and pulled her into his arms. This was one of her favorite places in the whole entire world. Comfort enveloped her as she inhaled his scent. The comfort was fleeting as she opened her eyes.

Pulling back, she quickly forced out. "Arn, a human has been captured, and we believe brought here. I'm afraid someone here means him harm. Please help us find him."

Arn nodded, but then his dark eyes regarded Henry and frowned. "Who are you?"

Henry made a move to answer, but Serena stopped him. "I'll explain later, please, Arn! Help me find Jack."

"Jack? This is the human you know?" Arn asked, disbelieving. His face was tight with confusion and apprehension.

"Yes. I do know him. I love him, and he loves me. Please, help me find him and keep him from harm."

"But Rahfey...the Overseers have pledged you to him."

"I'm not Rahfey's, I never was. I'm Jack's. I will always be Jack's, no matter what happens."

"The Overseers will kill you and the human for this," Arn said gravely, almost hushed. "You need to leave, quickly. Go to the north; there is a clan who will take you—"

"I don't care! Please, Arn! Help me! I won't leave without Jack. I'd rather die." Serena grabbed a hold of his arm to drag him out of the room.

Arn seemed to consider this for a moment and then nodded.

"Okay." Arn led her out, his heavy feet pounding the walkway. Serena and Henry followed closely behind as he steered them downward to another path that headed to more quarters.

Chapter 38: **Serena**

Following Arn, Serena wondered why he was heading the way he was, because he was leading them to the Overseers' meeting room. It was where they gathered and talked over issues about the Siege when they came up. Surely, Jack would not be there.

When they entered the room, it was like a trial was occurring. All the Overseers sat at the far end, and a crowd stood on the other side. Four figures were in the middle. Rahfey and two men holding a kneeling man.

Jack, still in his fire pants and suspenders.

Serena started to run, but Arn held her back. She tried to break free, but Arn was stronger than she was.

He leaned over and whispered, "Wait."

Serena stared over at Jack and studied him, mentally calculating his injuries. Except for a black eye and some blood on his mouth, he appeared okay. When they made eye contact, he struggled against his captors' grips to stand, but was violently pushed back down to his knees. He shot her a look, so she tried to reassure him with her hands and a look.

"What is this?" Baden bellowed, as they burst into the room.

"I could ask you the same thing," Arn replied dryly. "What are you doing to this human male?"

Baden's face reddened. "You have no right to question what the Overseers do. Go back to your quarters!"

Serena glanced to Rahfey. His eyes burned with the most intense anger she had ever seen, and he stood facing her, his fists clenched. She sneered at him and tore her glare away.

"Everyone in this Siege has a right to ask what you are doing." Arn inched closer to the four men in the center of the room with an air of confidence. "This human should not be here. The fact he was kidnapped and brought here should be a violation of the law, and the one who did that should be punished accordingly." Arn stared at Baden, unyielding.

Serena wanted to run to Jack, to tear apart the men who held him. It was all she could do to force herself to breathe and trust what Arn was doing. He hadn't let her down before, and she just needed to trust him.

Baden laughed bitterly. "When a human breaks our laws and interferes with us, then he will be held to our laws accordingly."

"What could this human have done to warrant this?" Arn challenged.

Before Baden could answer, Rahfey yelled, "This human encroached on my mating! He has sullied my female!"

"*What?*" Serena shouted involuntarily.

All eyes turned to her. But she held her ground, not wanting to show any weakness. She slowly approached Rahfey. Henry and Arn moved with her, which gave her more courage to continue.

"This human did not sully me, and further, I am not your mate!"

"She's mine," Jack answered, his expression furious and scornful.

Rahfey backhanded Jack in response. Serena saw red, rushing Rahfey at the same time Henry did. Arn caught her before she reached him, but no one could get to Henry.

Henry roared and delivered a blow that sent Rahfey across the room. Rahfey landed hard against the rocks, but he was up in a moment and rushed back at Henry. The two collided like boulders, ferocious growls emanating from them.

While they fought, Serena broke free of Arn and pushed one male off Jack. To her surprise, Arn freed him from the other. Each of them helped Jack up. He leaned over and kissed the side of her head.

"I prayed you wouldn't come; I didn't want you back here."

Serena stared up into his blue eyes. "I could never be kept from you."

He smiled faintly. "I couldn't be kept from you either."

Their reunion was interrupted by shouting as Henry and Rahfey were pulled apart.

"Enough!" Baden yelled, his voice reverberating off the walls. "We'll have no more disruption!"

Henry's shirt was torn and there was some blood on his arm, but other than that, he seemed fine.

"Hold the newcomer to our Siege. We'll deal with him in a moment," Baden urged, and the men went for Henry. He fought hard, but in the end, there were just too many of them. He had to yield or he'd be killed.

"Damn, I didn't know Henry had it in him," Jack murmured.

"There is a lot about him you don't know," Serena replied.

Once order was restored, Baden stood and faced a panting Rahfey. "What do you demand as the wronged mate for this encroachment?"

Serena pulled Jack closer; she wasn't going to let him go again. And if she died defending him, so be it. He was hers, and she was his. Nothing was going to keep them apart, ever.

"I demand recompense. I demand his death," Rahfey spat.

Baden didn't bat an eye. But before he could pronounce the sentence, Serena knew she needed to say something.

Moving out from Jack, she loudly declared, "I have mated this human male. We have consummated our union in a blood binding as required by our laws. He now has rights here in this gathering as my true mate. I was never going to agree to be Rahfey's when I was given to him by the Overseers without my consent." She turned to Baden. "And by you, Anaximander. Maybe you should have consulted me first before you made that decision."

There was a collective gasp in the room as she made the pronouncement. Glancing around, she could see members of her clan whispering and murmuring. This was it, and there was no going back. Even though it was a lie, it was the only thing she thought could work. She only hoped Jack and Arn would go along with it.

"What?" Rahfey asked, almost deathly quiet. "You gave yourself to him?" He inched closer to her. "You are mine. How could you give yourself to a human? It's an abomination."

Serena stared into his eyes, hating everything about him. She wished she could take her fingers, gouge out his eyes, and feed them to him.

"I chose him. After you beat me unconscious, I went and pledged myself to him, and we have consummated it. It cannot be undone."

She knew what she said could bring a harsh punishment on her, but she couldn't let Rahfey think he owned her in any way. If they assumed she belonged to Jack, they would end this trial and could turn her out forever, shunning her and making her an outcast. It was a small price to pay if they left Jack alone.

"It was him? He was the one who beat you?" Jack roared, and Serena could hear him struggling behind her. She hadn't revealed specifically who had whipped her raw because she knew Jack would want to retaliate. She couldn't risk it so she kept the detail to herself.

Jack screamed, "I'll kill you! You worthless piece of meat, I will kill you where you stand! Let me go!"

Serena tried to reassure him. "It's okay, Jack. I'm healed, I'm here, and he won't touch me again."

"Damn straight!" Jack yelled. "Because I will break every bone in his body."

"If you don't, I will," Henry chimed in, still breathing heavy.

"How very touching," Rahfey sneered, glancing between them. His body was coiled as if ready to jump at either one.

Serena reached into the collar of Jack's shirt and pulled out her Shilund insignia, letting it rest against his chest in clear view of everyone. Excited murmurs erupted as she walked back to face Rahfey.

"We are mated."

Rahfey shouted a curse, but he was interrupted by Baden.

"Silence!" Baden shouted, stroking his thick, red beard as he paced. "This does change things." He turned to Rahfey. "You could still demand recompense for the loss of the female."

"That is all he can demand, but this human cannot be condemned to death," Arn clarified.

Rahfey reluctantly looked to Baden, confused at first, and then a sickly smile crept across his narrow face.

"I demand combat with my offender." Rahfey looked over to Jack. Serena wasn't sure, but she thought she saw him lick his lips.

"No!" she protested. Jack could not win against Rahfey. No human was a match against a Shilund's massive strength. The battle would kill Jack, and she knew it.

Henry yelled to her, "Can he do that?"

Serena nodded then turned to Rahfey. "Why are you doing this? You know he cannot stand against you. This is so dishonorable of you to demand this of someone obviously weaker than a Shilund!"

Rahfey sneered. "He chose to mate a Shilund, and so he should be expected to act as one, including abiding by our laws. But with the Rights of Exchange, you could take his place in the fight and defend your male. It's rather fitting his female defend him. Really, Serena, to be with one so weak, it does not become you."

She stared at Rahfey in disgust. Taking in a deep breath, she slowly turned to Jack and took his face in her hands, "Jack, listen to me. He is a Shilund and you are human. His strength is far beyond yours. It doesn't make you weak; I know you are a strong male in the human world but here it's a different story. Please, you can choose a representative to take your place in the fight. Pick me to take your place; you know I am as strong as he is. Please, I have more of a chance."

"No, Serena," he huffed, his temper still rolling. "I want to kill him for touching you."

"I know." She stroked his face. "But please don't do this. I love you, and I want you to live."

"I will not let you take my place and allow him to touch you again. Absolutely not!"

"Let me," a strong voice echoed in the tense silence.

Serena and Jack both turned and looked at Henry. They stared at him, dumbfounded.

"No!" Jack roared. "This isn't your fight, and I want his blood."

"Sure it is. As long as you are my friend, it will be my fight. I can do this, Jack. Let me stand in for you."

"I can't let either one of you do this for me." Jack's eyes burned hot as he stared at her. "I know it doesn't look like I can do this, but I want to defend you, to defend us."

Serena dropped to her knees. "Please, Jack. Please, please, don't do this. There is no dishonor as a male to elect another on your behalf. Our laws allow for it."

Before she knew it, Henry was beside her. "Jack, I am one of them. I stand a strong chance of winning. Let me represent you both in this fight."

Jack and Henry looked at each other, unspoken words passing between them.

"You are one of them? A Shilund?"

Henry nodded.

"Well, I'll be. Guess it explains the freaky eyes," Jack muttered under his breath. "But I don't want anyone to take my place, ever. I want to kill him, do you understand? I want him to pay for all the pain he has caused Serena and for killing Chris and Adam. I can more than deliver the pain he deserves."

Henry's eyes darkened. "He killed Chris and Adam?"

"Yes, he admitted it to me on the way here. So, you see, I owe him."

Serena rose to her feet and Henry's face grew dark.

Henry leaned in closer to Jack. "Then this is absolutely my fight, too. Let me avenge them."

Jack started to waver.

Henry continued, "I know you're not afraid. But he is hellishly strong, and I want you to live. You need to be with Serena, and you can't do that if he kills you. Just let me try. Let me take your place."

"No. This is my right."

Serena and Henry stared Jack down. He crossed his arms in protest, but seemed unyielding.

How could she make him understand? He was strong, beautiful, and no doubt, he could give Rahfey a good fight, but he would undoubtedly die. Her heart clenched tight, and she thought she might double over from the pain of it.

"Please, Jack. I'm begging you. If you love me, if you want us to be together, please use the exchange. For me. Please."

A war played out on his face. He sighed and turned his eyes down. "Fine. Whatever. For this fight, okay. But it won't be you. And know, I will kick his ass, if not here and now, it will be later, and I won't give that up for anything."

"Okay." Serena let out a heavy breath. She turned to Henry. She didn't know him, and didn't know if he had fighting ability, but he was a Shilund and stood a chance against Rahfey.

Arn interjected. "Newcomer, I can take the human's place in this fight." Arn studied Henry and waited.

Henry lifted his hands in protest. "No, it'll be me."

"Are you females going to start kissing each other or would one of you like to join me here to die by my hand?" Rahfey challenged with his arms crossed. A few Shilund males behind him chuckled in agreement.

Jack rushed toward Rahfey, but Serena stopped him with a hand to his chest. "You and I are going to tangle. Count on it," Jack huffed.

"Here I am." Rahfey spread his arms wide in a mocking protest. "If you would just quit hiding behind your female we could get down to it."

Henry turned to a fuming Jack. "Pick me, Jack. God! Give me an opportunity to put him in his place." Rahfey saw the exchange and laughed.

Jack seemed to calm and shook his head. "You are such a head case, but okay. You can take my place. But you better kick his ass and I mean good."

Henry grinned. "You can pay me back for this later. Steak dinners every week till I'm fifty sounds like a fair trade."

Jack grumbled under his breath before shaking hands with

Henry. "Just don't kill him. Maim, sure, permanently disfigure, I'd love to see it. But killing, I want that honor."

"No promises," Henry said with a smile.

Jack glanced to Arn. "Thank you for the offer, but it looks like Henry's the replacement." Arn nodded once and then faced Rahfey and Baden.

"I choose Henry to take my place," Jack choked out.

Baden dipped his head in approval, and then addressed the crowd. "Recompense in the main corridor! May the best male win."

The crowd cheered and took off in all directions as Jack, Serena, Henry, and Arn watched. Jack snuck his arm around Serena's waist and kissed her head.

"I hope you know what you're doing," Jack whispered to Henry.

"Nope."

"Great. We got the blind leading the human," Jack huffed as he took Serena's hand and followed the others to a different room.

Chapter 39: Devon

Devon knew something was up when he saw the good deputy tear out of town like a bat out of hell with a girl he had never seen before. Afraid of possibly missing a sighting of the animal or thing or whatever, he decided to follow the deputy and his raven-haired sidekick.

The deputy drove so quickly he almost couldn't keep up, but fortunately, Devon didn't lose him. He wasn't surprised when the deputy made his way into the deep forest and parked along the road. Devon kept his car some distance away and pulled along the side of the road, obscured by some brush.

The trunk light of the police cruiser illuminated the deputy as he took off his shirt and gun belt, put them in, and closed the lid. Something was definitely up, and Devon was going to find out. Thankfully, he had one camera he could take pictures with and slung it around his neck. He thought idly how his appearance was like some psycho tourist with a death wish. The thought made him chuckle.

Finally, the deputy stuck a gun in the back of his pants, and he and his little companion started into the woods. Devon grabbed his night-vision goggles and got out of his car. He crouched down so he wouldn't be spotted as he prepared to follow them.

The girl and the deputy didn't say much to one another, but walked along silently as if in deep thought. Devon wouldn't be able to talk either if he were trailing behind that sweet little morsel of a woman. He'd be too distracted by her swaying as she walked. But the deputy didn't seem to take notice; he simply moved along the woods, determined toward an unknown goal.

They walked along for what seemed like hours until they stopped in some brush. Immediately, Devon paused and saw an exchange of words between the beauty and the deputy. Devon couldn't make out the words, but their conversation was quick, and then they set off again. They walked to the base of a particularly large hill, which was densely covered with plant life, so much so that in the pale moonlight, it resembled a black blanket.

The pair went into the dense brush and just before he was about to enter, he heard the woman exclaim, "Do not harm the Shilund with me. His father is of our clan and he has a right to be here."

Shilund? What's a Shilund?

Devon couldn't make those words fit into any context he could come up with. Was the woman talking about the fine Deputy Henry Parrish? And what was a Shilund? His senses tingled, and he knew he was on the verge of something big. His mouth almost salivated.

Creeping into the black brush, he could make out the deputy and the woman heading up the hill and pausing on a little rise about halfway up. He watched and waited. The woman reached out to touch some vines when three men descended from the trees and grabbed them.

Devon lifted his camera. Thank God he thought to set it to night photography before he left his car. He lifted it and began snapping photos of the group.

Who were those men and how did they so easily drop from the trees? They must be trained military like him. But why were they out here anyway? Probably guarding something top secret. The military was known for hiding stuff in very odd places. He moved as quickly as he could to the base of the hill while everyone was distracted.

He watched in odd fascination as the men that held Deputy Parrish and the girl completely backed off when he showed them something, probably his badge. It was almost like a magic pass into anywhere.

Suddenly, the deputy and the girl were gone. *Poof!* Into thin air right into the side of the hill. He theorized there must be a hidden entrance, and now he wanted even more to find out what was there. It was big, to be sure.

The men in the trees had a great vantage point and getting around them was going to be difficult at best. He figured the only way to make it up the hill was to move slowly so that he wouldn't cause too much disruption to the vegetation around him.

As he moved, his mind wandered to the many reports he had read in the library, documenting various odd accidents and strange sightings in the woods. By themselves, they could have been dismissed, but add them all together, and it was evident that something was out here. But was it a new type of animal, a super freak of nature, or a perversion of a normal animal? Heaven forbid it was actually a Sasquatch. If it were, he wouldn't make any type of claims along those lines unless he had hard proof. He wasn't going to let his show *Fringe Hunter* be associated with those backward peons who had a show on the competing channel claiming a Bigfoot was around every corner. He couldn't stand the fact they made all legitimate investigators look bad.

Fifteen arduous minutes passed by, and he realized he had gotten all of ten feet. This wasn't working. Whatever was happening up there was going to pass him by while he moved like a snail. To his surprise and great relief, all three men suddenly dropped from the trees and went in the same way as the deputy and the girl.

He waited for them to come back out and after a few moments of nothing, he stood and ran full force up the hill. The soil gave in a few places, and he slipped and almost fell, recovering before he did a face plant. Deftly, he made it up to the opening, pausing outside to listen. He heard nothing of significance. Reaching out, he pushed back the vines and inched in.

Standing frozen just inside the entrance, he waited for his eyes to adjust so that he could continue. He stood on a high rock ledge, overlooking a large open area below, like a small amphitheater. Hundreds of people were here, dressed in leather and the oddest eclectic style of clothing he had ever seen. They stood in a large circle around a small group in the middle. Devon immediately crouched down to hide behind the rocks and watch. He was thankful for the murmuring because it camouflaged the clicks of his camera as he took one shot after another.

Recognizing Jack Day, he cursed to himself. It was the guy who had been hurt out here when the two were killed weeks ago. *Jerk*. He must know more than he'd said. It wasn't that surprising. He knew Jack had been holding something back. With Jack was the girl he'd seen earlier. Standing close to them was another extremely large man with dark hair and Henry Parrish.

The deputy was shirtless, his muscles bulging and coiled, holding himself in a stance like he was ready to fight, dancing on the balls of his feet like a boxer. Across from him was a dark-haired man about Henry's age, dressed in the same strange clothing as the others. That man removed his shirt, and Devon noted he was just as muscular and lean as Henry Parrish was.

Devon realized there was going to be a fight and turned the dial on his camera to film mode. As he gazed through the camera at the opponent of Henry's, his heart stopped. The man had canines like a leopard's. What the heck was he? A rush of fear spiked through him, but he held his position and kept filming.

Well, Alice, welcome to the rabbit hole.

Chapter 40: **Henry**

Henry steadily watched as Rahfey growled and swore profanities at him, telling him how he was going to kill him. Henry wasn't afraid even in the slightest. His human father had constantly warned him to keep his strength hidden from everyone and now that part of him prowled around like a lion inside wanting out. The lion wanted to destroy this Rahfey character.

The martial arts he had taken growing up and his police training made him fully ready for whatever this little wimp was going to sling his way.

It was funny, but he felt like he belonged here on some kind of indefinable level. For the first time in his life, he was a part of the world around him. Being adopted by his human parents was a true Godsend, but he never felt entirely a part of human life. He was always a consummate outsider.

Add in the fact that his mother's clan had rejected him a second time when he sought them out after he graduated high school. He knew he would be an eternal outcast to everyone and everything around him. He didn't realize how left out he'd felt until this very moment. The lonely Leif that trolled around on the inside of his head was relieved at being among those who were like him. The exhilaration of it all, mixed with his adrenaline, almost gave him a high.

Rahfey was making a show of it, raising his hands and getting the crowd excited and cheering. No matter, Henry didn't care what they thought about him. Henry knew he'd win this fight. He just wished Rahfey would realize it and stop acting like such a diva.

Baden, the bearded wonder, approached Henry and Rahfey and motioned them forth. Henry and Rahfey mirrored each other as they took their places before Baden.

Baden acted like a ringmaster, full of spit and vinegar. "We are here today to allow Rahfey rights of recompense for the interloper claiming his intended. However, we Shilund are not without understanding, and so the interloper is allowed to defend himself in this combat. If the challenged one is deformed or at a disadvantage," Baden glared pointedly at Jack, "then he can choose a representative to fight on his behalf."

Baden pointed toward Henry. "This outsider has been selected to represent the human Jack."

Henry hated how Baden sneered at him and pronounced his words like a grand orator. He looked Baden straight in his eyes and did not even blink. He was not intimidated by any of them.

Baden turned to the crowd for a moment and then to Rahfey. "Rahfey, please show your lineage as a Shilund."

Rahfey took off a necklace that was tied close to his neck. He stood before Baden, showing him the insignia. As he walked over to the Overseers, he lifted it up and slowly showed them. Each Overseer nodded. Rahfey handed his insignia to another Shilund who waited along the outer portion of the crowd.

Too bad, I would have loved to choke him with that.

"Show your lineage as a Shilund," Baden demanded, indicating Henry.

Henry fished out the insignia he had carried his whole life, the one thing that tied him to his true identity. He never understood its significance and wasn't sure what it said or meant, but he remembered his mother saying to him before she died that it was who he was. He never realized she had meant it literally.

The circular, smooth silver symbol felt as if it weighed a hundred pounds as he pulled it out and showed it to Baden. He watched Baden's face turn pale and his lips draw into a tight line beneath the beard. He looked as if he was going to be sick. His eyes met Henry's and filled with fear. Henry furrowed his brows and turned to Serena, hoping for some understanding. To his surprise, she was grinning.

This took him back for a moment, but he forced himself to walk over to the Overseers and show them in the same manner as Rahfey.

A lot of whispering started, and some stared in disbelief. What was this thing he was holding and why did it seem to have such a strange effect on everyone? It was like holding a talisman of some sort. He just wished he knew what it was.

Returning to Serena, he handed it to her so it wouldn't get lost in the fight. Serena smiled up at him and wrapped it in her hands. Henry then shook Jack's hand.

Jack looked at him and smirked. "All this for steak. You sure know how to make a scene."

"You know a man needs to eat." Henry chuckled.

Just before Devon turned away, Arn's outstretched hand caught his eye. Henry took it, feeling the firm shake returned.

"Fight well, Henry," Arn bid with a nod.

"Thank you, sir," Henry replied, letting some of his police training peek through. Everyone was sir or ma'am.

Rahfey seemed apprehensive, and Baden's expression soured as if he had eaten thumbtacks. But no matter, Henry wanted this over with. Oddly, Vivienne filled his head at that moment and he wondered what she was doing while he was standing here.

A lone thought occurred to him that if he died, he wouldn't get to go out with her, and that seemed tragic.

I hope I see you again, Vivienne.

He was going to make good on the promise to ask her out. She was pretty and had a razor-sharp wit. The best part was that even though she had found out he was a Shilund, she still wanted the date. His expectations of being alone for the rest of his life were fading away in this very peculiar hope. He had always stayed very far from human women because he couldn't risk being discovered as different. And now, there was this real possibility of hanging out with a beautiful girl and just being himself.

Focus, Henry! Focus.

Rahfey glared at him, cracking his knuckles, almost drooling at the chance to fight. Henry was right there with him.

A short male brought a knife to Rahfey, handed it to him, turned to Henry, handed him one, and darted off to the side. Henry measured the weight of the knife in his hands and tested the sharpness. It would cut through skin very easily. Yeah, no injury to maim here, they were expected to kill. Such a warming thought.

Right before they were to start, Henry's eyes moved to Baden and he was shocked to see him looking...what was it...was it panic? Yes, Baden appeared afraid.

Chapter 41: Jack

Jack held Serena against him as they backed up to stand with the rest of the crowd. Her body was shaking slightly, and he guessed it was possibly out of fear, or was it fury? He wondered idly if it was out of the same sort of intense anger he had for Rahfey. Henry might be representing him in this fight, but he would pay Rahfey back. Every lash, every drop of blood, every tear that was cried by Serena. This battle wasn't settling anything for him. This was merely to satisfy some of the Shilund's twisted sense of honor.

He was shoulder to shoulder with Arn. Arn was such a likable guy, never mind that he was Serena's father. His presence was commanding but calm. He seemed like a leader, certainly not a follower. Jack liked him immediately. He hoped they could have a more proper introduction once all of this was over. He glanced at Arn, and his brown eyes were fixated on the arena where the fight would occur. He could see a tick working in Arn's jaw. Arn must not like this any more than he did.

Jack prayed that Henry would be okay. They had been friends a long time, and he thought a lot of him. Henry always kept most people at arm's length on a certain level, but now that made sense.

Watching Henry prepare for the fight, Jack thought it seemed he had been among them his entire life. Henry's body was cut, strong, and glowed with a slight sheen of sweat on his exposed upper body. It reminded Jack of the MMA fights he had watched a few times on Pay-Per-View. Except now, there was no referee and Jack feared how one was declared the winner. Oh God, what had he allowed Henry to do standing in his place? A sickly guilt wrapped him over his powerlessness to stop all of it.

He pulled Serena closer and kissed her head. She smelled of sweet pine, and it calmed a part of him. The half of him that had been missing was now here in his arms. He was never going to let her go, no matter what it cost him.

A fiery-headed woman came forward and raised her hands to quiet the crowd. A hush settled. She looked to Rahfey, then Henry, and motioned for them to begin.

They circled each other; Rahfey huddled down like a tight coil ready to spring. His movement was fluid and sure as he stepped side-to-side, assessing Henry.

Henry, by contrast, was steadily holding his knife, not grimacing, but calmly looking Rahfey over. He was slightly lower to the ground, his movements more measured. Jack couldn't tell if it was a good thing or bad.

Rahfey made the first move, thrusting forward toward Henry's midsection, but he was batted to the side. Where the blow may have knocked down a lesser man, Rahfey simply shifted his weight and turned, bringing up his blade and narrowly missing Henry.

Rahfey recovered and circled Henry. They moved together in a deadly dance. Henry shifted the blade to his other hand and smirked at Rahfey.

Rahfey's face morphed into a mask of anger, but he quickly recovered. He rushed Henry as if he were going to strike the same way, but a split second before he should have thrust forward, he dropped to his side and swept Henry's legs out from under him, tumbling him to the ground.

Serena lunged forward, but Jack and Arn held her back.

Henry landed on his front, but swiftly rolled out of reach as Rahfey plunged his blade hard into the ground beneath him. Henry brought the back of his hand into Rahfey's head and then leapt on his back, sinking his blade into his shoulder.

Rahfey let out a loud bellow of pain, but he managed to rise with Henry on his back. He slammed him on the ground while he landed on top, but he lost grip of his blade. He scurried off Henry to recover it, but Henry was able to regain his previous position on his back before Rahfey could reach it, his arm around his neck, the crook of his elbow creating the perfect noose.

Rahfey gripped Henry's arm in a grimace, trying to suck in air but successfully. His elbow slammed into Henry's midsection, once, twice, and finally on the third try, it succeeded in loosening Henry's grip.

Rahfey twisted and punched Henry hard in the face. Blood shot out like a flood from his nose. Jack supposed that must have broken it.

Henry briefly touched it, and then jumped to his feet, his bloody blade still gripped in his hand.

Rahfey made it to his own blade and stood, again assessing Henry. Blood was running down his back from the gaping wound in his shoulder, but he appeared undaunted. Rahfey rushed forward to strike again, and as Henry prepared to grab his arm, Rahfey scooped up a handful of dust and threw it into Henry's eyes, effectively blinding him.

"No!" Baden shouted.

Rahfey sprang forward and shoved Henry through the crowd into the farthest stone wall, preparing to cut Henry's throat. Just before the blade made contact, Henry managed to grab Rahfey's arm and hold it back.

Time stood still as Henry held Rahfey's arm back from his throat—it slowly inched forward, getting closer to his jugular.

"Henry!" Serena shouted.

Jack's feet were anchored in place as he watched his friend about to be killed.

The blade touched Henry's neck and right before Rahfey could push it deeper in, Henry brought his knee up into Rahfey's midsection. An *oof* sounded from Rahfey, and he doubled over, unable to breathe as he dropped his blade.

Henry threw his knife to the side and swiped at the dirt in his eyes. He blinked a few times, lunged for Rahfey, and pushed him onto his back, bringing down his fist over and over into Rahfey's face. Rahfey was ineffectual in stopping the rain of fists battering his head and finally was of no threat to Henry.

Henry rolled off Rahfey and struggled to his feet. He staggered like a drunken man to retrieve the blade on the ground. He picked it up, turned back to Rahfey, and stood over him. Except instead of driving the knife down, he just stood there, breathing heavily and staring at him.

"Kill!" someone yelled. Everything was silent for a moment, and then it came from different parts of the crowd. Then in unison, the demand rose. "Kill! Kill! Kill!"

Henry searched around the cavern, listening to the chant, his sweaty chest heaving from exertion. Glancing down at the blade in his hand, he paused, and then brought the blade down with all his might at Rahfey's head.

Silence. No one moved. Henry was leaning over Rahfey's body, and then he slowly stood straight. He rounded on Baden and the Overseers, panting hard.

"I win." He held out his arms as if in presenting himself to them. He waited for the confirmation of it from them.

Jack saw the blade handle, except it wasn't buried in Rahfey's head. It was impaled in the ground an inch beside it. He had spared

Rahfey's life.

Baden set out for Henry, when suddenly a cry sounded and Rahfey rushed forward, blade in hand, coming at Henry's back. Before he made it, Baden threw a blade to Henry, who turned and buried it into Rahfey's midsection as he reached him.

Rahfey's face was a mask of confusion and pain. He held onto Henry's shoulders and got close to his face. "Now...you win." Rahfey crumpled to the ground and didn't move.

Henry looked down at the body of Rahfey, but his face gave nothing away. Jack watched as Henry walked slowly back to him and Serena.

They both ran to him with Arn, Arn taking one side of Henry and Jack taking the other. They led him to a seat, letting him sit and rest. Serena brought some water to him and kneeled at his feet.

"Are you okay?" Serena asked.

Henry took a drink with heavy breathing and then used his hand to wipe the blood from his face. "Never better." He laughed a sarcastic laugh. Then he patted her on the shoulder. "I'm okay. Now you guys should be free to be together. Right?"

Arn spoke up. "Well, Serena is freed from Rahfey, but not necessarily free to be with Jack."

Jack couldn't believe what he was hearing. "What? Do you mean, they would try to keep us apart?"

Arn shook his head. "I'm not sure what is going to happen at this point. We've not had a human and Shilund join before, so I don't have the answer as to how the Overseers will treat this."

Before Jack could respond, Baden made his way over. "This male has won on behalf of Serena and Jack. The recompense is completed."

Jack tugged Serena closer and held her tight. This was over, or so he hoped.

Serena leaned away from Jack, reached up, kissed him, and smiled. "I love you," she whispered.

"I love you, too," he replied, gazing into her golden eyes.

Serena smiled and then reached into her pocket, producing Henry's insignia. She handed it to him.

Serena began, "Leif, this—" she pointed to Baden "—is your father, Baden."

Henry was dumbfounded. Eventually, he stood up and stared into Baden's green eyes. Jack realized their eyes were the same color.

"What?" Jack could not believe his ears. Baden had been Rahfey's partner this entire time, wanting Jack dead, and was like the grand ringleader of this would-be execution. And he was Henry's father? Unbelievable.

Henry gazed at Baden, not saying a word. Baden held out his hand to Henry. It seemed like hours went by before Henry finally accepted it, shaking his hand. But he didn't smile or seem all that pleased.

Arn handed Henry his T-shirt and the guns he had been wearing before the fight. Henry accepted them, putting on the shirt and stowing the guns.

Serena pulled on Jack's arm and led him away from Baden and Henry. The crowd dispersed slowly, each Shilund going their way. The show was over.

Arn waved to Serena and Jack as they walked to the side. Serena smiled at him and waved back.

Serena jumped into Jack's arms. "Now, you'll never be able to get rid of me." She wrapped her arms around him and kissed him.

Jack loved how she felt there. He pulled her closer and kissed her deeply. He couldn't imagine how he got lucky enough to have her as his own. But he'd take it and thank God every moment for her.

"I think you have that wrong. You'll never be able to get rid of me." He chuckled against her lips.

"Guess we are stuck with each other." She found his mouth again, gently, achingly slow, and kissed him into oblivion.

When Jack eventually pulled back, he watched the Shilund men gather up the body of Rahfey. He wasn't sure why, but Rahfey's death wasn't enough. It had been too easy, in fact. It should have been him that delivered the killing blow and not Henry. He had to force himself to focus on Serena. She was in his arms and whole and safe. No one was going to hurt her again, not as long as he breathed air. But still, it bothered him that Rahfey's death at Henry's hands seemed a little like a failure on his part.

Serena took his hand and led him away.

Chapter 42: Devon

Devon couldn't believe what he had just watched. The good Deputy Parrish had just killed a man...or whatever that thing was, right before his eyes. And as fate would have it, it was all recorded. Now, no one could dispute this. There were people, or some sort of race, living in these woods, apart from humans. He was sure they were the reason the two men were killed not far from here weeks ago.

Devon decided it was probably best if he got the heck out of there. After putting the camera safely in his pocket and still hunched over, he slowly moved to the entrance of the cave.

He was almost giddy at the thought of the amount of validation he would get from this. His name would go down in history as having made one of the biggest discoveries of all time. He was a regular Columbus. It made him smile. Maybe this was enough to redeem him for the past. He hoped so.

As he moved closer to the entrance of the cave, he caught sight of two feet beside him. Trailing his eyes up the body, he met the face of a grimacing man with cat-like eyes. He sneered, exposing the longest canines Devon had ever seen. Before he could respond, the man struck him with a boot to the face. The last thing he saw was stars.

Epilogue

One week later...

It was cool in the late afternoon, the sun just having retreated over the roof of Jack's house, casting a long shadow over his backyard patio.

Four figures sat there, relaxing after having eaten. Serena was in Jack's lap, and Vivienne and Henry sat in chairs near them.

Vivienne had maneuvered her chair as close to Henry as she could without climbing into his lap. She would lean in and smile at him shyly. Henry didn't seem to mind.

"So, what are you going to do now?" Jack asked of Henry as his hand trailed lazily over Serena's arm.

Henry studied the drink he held in his hand. "I'm not really sure. Baden wants me to come to the Siege and live, but I told him no. I'm not ready for something like that."

"Did he tell you of your mother?" Serena questioned as she let herself caress the back of Jack's neck.

Henry shook his head and continued to look at his drink. Serena thought how lost he seemed in that moment.

"He said he'd tell me soon. But that it was a long story and not one he wanted to get into right now." Henry shrugged. "But it's okay, I know that Dorothy Parrish is my mother. So, details about Anisa are not important to me right now."

Vivienne patted Henry's arm in comfort. Henry smiled, took her hand, and squeezed reassuringly.

Henry turned to look at her and Jack. "What about you two? What is the pronouncement from the Overseers?"

"Yeah?" Vivienne matched.

"Well," Serena began, "they are allowing the relationship for the moment. They believe we have mated so they won't keep us from each other, as long as we keep the Shilund a secret. For now, that is their only requirement."

"For now? Could it change?" Vivienne asked.

Serena nodded as she sat up. "Yes. They don't know what to do about us, and so I have a feeling it could change if they feel we threaten the clan or any Shilund. I don't think they've ever been faced with a Shilund mating a human. They don't know what to do when two of our laws contradict each other, because mating is very sacred. However, they may decide we still violate the original law of having contact and condemn us both."

Jack pulled Serena to him, snuggling close to her. "That's not going to happen, and they won't ever keep us apart."

Serena lifted her hands and rubbed his cheek. "No, my love, no one will ever keep us apart."

She leaned in and captured his lips as her insides burst with excitement. She would be with Jack forever, regardless of anyone or anything.

* * *

It was midnight when a black SUV drove slowly into Presque Isle, right down Main Street. It made no pause until it reached the Hotel Hideaway on the edge of town. The vehicle pulled up to the door of the room rented by Devon Hennessey and sat parked with its engine running. The opaque windows revealed nothing about the occupants inside.

Eventually, the SUV door opened, and a woman dressed in black and with a gun strapped to her side stepped out and looked around cautiously. Her brown hair was cropped short to her head like a man's, and she wore obsidian shades. Everything about her screamed military.

A man exited the passenger side, dressed in the same attire, and shut his door. They made their way to the door of the room and searched around for anyone who might be looking.

Shoving a jimmy into the jamb, the man forced the door open with little effort. Within seconds, they slipped in and closed the door.

The man scanned the room full of closed circuit TVs and recording equipment. He opened the drawers and rifled through them, looking for any indication as to what the reporters had found.

"Command has said more men are coming our way if we need it," the woman said as she removed her dark glasses and placed them on the dresser.

"Tell them to send a recon group so we can review what the reporters uncovered with these cameras," the man reaffirmed. "There is a pocket of the animals here. I'm sure the doctor will be interested."

"Yes, sir," the woman replied, and began to text.

Acknowledgments

Thank you God for your faithfulness and for keeping all of your promises.

Thank you to Liz Joseph! It means the world to me that you took such time to review and edit this. I'm blessed to call you friend.

Thank you to Kristen Engelhardt, for helping me out early on. Your hard work did not go unnoticed.

Thank you to Sherrie Henry and Johanna Rae, for always encouraging me to write and be true to who I was no matter what others thought.

Thank you to Lis, Tonia, Kim, Christy aka Tink and Tyia! Thanks for being a great group of beta readers.

Thank you to Dawn Edwards for being the best friend a girl could have. Your daily texts helped me get through every moment of life! Good times, bad times, you have always been there and had my back.

Kierdan, Kayleigh, Landon, Aiden and Billy, I love you.

Sneak peek - Torn

Book 2 of The Shilund Saga

Chapter 1 - Devon

Rocks bit hard into Devon Hennessey's cheek as he lay face down. The heaviness holding his eyes closed told him he was blindfolded. His hands and feet were bound tightly behind him, and he couldn't move. As he slowly regained consciousness, he tried to remember why he lay there and why his hands and feet were tied. Was he still in Afghanistan? Had insurgents caught him? Were they preparing to execute him in front of a video camera for the world to see? God knew he was worthy of it for things he had done while working for the Red Ops.

His brain was hazy. Where he was? He slowly moved his fingers back and forth to try to regain some feeling in them, but it didn't help. They were so numb, they seemed as if they'd been chopped off.

How had the Taliban caught him? He kept as still as he could and thought hard about where he had been before they had captured him. He had been doing…what? Why was it so hard to remember?

He wanted to try to shift his weight to take the pressure off his hips, but that would alert the insurgents that he was awake. God forbid they discover that and start an interrogation.

The air smelled earthy and had an acrid odor that told him he was in a cave and not in a building. If they wanted to execute him in the mountains, fine. He'd go down fighting once they were ready to start. If they were in the mountains, that meant he was probably miles away from his unit and miles away from a rescue, hidden in one of the millions of grottos that dotted the landscape of Afghanistan.

He accepted he was probably getting what was due to him. After all, he had been working with the Red Ops for months now, smuggling out captives to Wyoming for his superiors to do God knew what to them; shipping them in crates like books. He never knew what was in store for those captives, but he had never asked either. The prisoners had always been unconscious when they were sent out of

Afghanistan, so he was spared their accusing eyes.

Maybe whoever had him now were relatives of those captives. If so, maybe they would want to exchange him for some of those smuggled out. He hoped so. As much as he wasn't afraid of them, or even to die, he didn't want to undergo any torture he was sure would come before the actual death.

Thinking of relatives reminded him of his own parents, and that was something he didn't even want to consider. It wasn't like he had two parents who actually cared what happened to him. Hell, he hadn't even talked to them in years. They lived in their own self-imposed torture after they divorced. When he had joined the military at eighteen and received notice of his first assignment, he made an effort to spend time with each of them in case he was killed in action, but that had fallen flat. His father didn't have time for him, and his mother simply sat with him, chain smoking and coughing, not interested in where he was going. So, he had left them and never went back. He wasn't even sure they were alive, but if they were and he were killed, he bet it wouldn't even make a dent in their miserable lives.

A soft female cough resounded. A girl was here? He had to make a decision; he could open his mouth and try to talk to her, or he could pretend to be asleep. Running all the scenarios through his head, he opted to talk and hoped to God she knew English.

Turning his head, a sharp pain radiated from his temple, and he realized he must have been struck there. Movement was a bad idea. His training had taught him to listen for subtle differences in the air density around him to know how to assess the amount of potential enemies to engage. He listened, but he could only hear one girl breathing.

Good. One is easier to deal with.

"Could I have some water?"

The figure move closer to him, and a smell caught his attention. She had food with her. His traitorous stomach growled, which did nothing to help his stance at defiance.

"Please, I'm very thirsty," Devon said again to try to garner sympathy. If he could convince her to loosen his hands, he'd break her neck and be out of here.

"Would you like to sit up first?" The small voice rang out from beside him in perfect unaccented English. Was she American? Or maybe she had gone to school in America.

"Yes. Would you be able to loosen my bindings so I could get some blood to my hands?"

Gentle hands helped him shift his weight into a sitting position. Pain tore through his legs and arms as some blood started to move, assailing him with a million pinpricks. God it hurt.

"I'm sorry, I can't touch your bindings. But I'll ask when they come back."

"When who comes back?"

"Eric and Magnar. They just left. Lean forward."

Eric and Magnar? Those were not Arab names. He was expecting Mohammad or Abdul, not Eric and Magnar.

"All right." He was hesitant, but he moved his body forward and waited. A cold metal cup greeted his lips as the water wash into his mouth. It was cool and refreshing, and before he knew it, he had drunk it all.

"More?" she asked.

"Yes," he said. Before he knew it, she removed the blindfold.

Blinking spastically, he attempted to focus on his surroundings. It was a small cavern with only one opening just past the blurry image of the girl. He could make out flaxen hair that fell just below her shoulders, which confused him. Her body was thin, and her skin pale. He wished he could get a better look at her.

While he was waiting for his second glass of water, two hulking figures approached. A fearful mewling noise escaped the girl's lips before she retreated to the farthest point in the cave.

"So the asshole is awake, I see," the larger of the two growled.

"Looks like," the other man agreed.

They didn't sound any more native than the girl did. The taller one had dark hair that stuck up in messy spikes. The second man had stringy dark blond hair, longer than the girl's. Both had short, unkempt beards. They must be Americans, all of them. Devon shoulders sagged at the thought.

"Eric and Magnar, I take it?" Devon's voice came out sharper than he liked. "Why the hell am I tied up? Unless you are traitors and are in with the Taliban. You must know I am an American soldier."

"Taliban?" The smaller man chuckled. "Cree? Did you give him tiperia?"

"Lay off him, Mag. He got hit pretty hard on the head," the larger man chided.

"Mm-hmm," Magnar replied stoically. He leaned against the wall and crossed his arms as Eric approached Devon.

"So, do you want to tell us what you were doing in our Siege?

With a camera, no less?"

Siege? Devon tried hard to remember where he had been last. Something about the word "camera" started needling at his mind. He shifted his weight against the jagged rock he leaned against.

Camera.

Camera.

Wait. He had been doing something with a camera…in a cave. Yes, he had been watching something. A fight?

A punch to the face had him lying on his side. Well, this must be the start of the interrogation. But, unlike the regular military, the Red Ops didn't have a protocol for how to handle being captured. You were just supposed to keep your pie hole closed.

"Answer me!" Eric screamed.

Devon spit out the blood and laughed. "Nice manners there, Eric."

The man got down at his level, breathing heavy. "How the hell do you know our names?" Devon was roughly pushed back, and his eyes began to focus. He could see long canines protruding from Eric's mouth. He wanted to scurry back out of Eric's reach, but couldn't.

Maybe I'm dreaming. I must still be unconscious.

"Hey man, your teeth are wicked wrong. Been to a dentist lately?"

Another blow sent him over to the side again. He tasted more blood in his mouth.

"Stop!" Cree shouted as she tried to rush forward, only to be held back by Magnar as he kept watch on the scene behind him.

"Oh no, Cree, you stay out of this." Magnar struggled to keep her back.

"But you are hurting him. Eric, please," she begged.

Devon could feel Eric grabbing a hold of his collar. He pulled hard, lifting Devon to sitting again. "Now, again I ask you, what were you doing in the Siege with a camera?"

God, this was going to get old quick.

Devon looked into his eyes and was startled. His pupils were like a cat's.

What the hell? I must have eaten something bad before I went to sleep. This is the weirdest dream ever.

"Bite me!" Devon spat in Eric's direction. Maybe it wasn't smart to say that to a…fanged man?…Mutant?…Reject from the Island of Dr. Moreau? Because he might actually do it.

"What the—" Eric shouted, and Devon knew he had hit his mark. This time Devon got kicked on his midsection. He doubled over, tasting dirt in his mouth from the cave floor.

"Please Eric! Stop!" Cree begged. Devon could make out a desperate tone in her voice that confused him. Why would she be concerned about him?

"Yeah Eric, I think Cree is right. I don't know how Baden will feel about us damaging him before he's had a chance to talk to him."

Baden? Then it started to come to him. Baden was the name of the man, the odd man, who oversaw a fight between the deputy and another man. Wait, he wasn't in Afghanistan. He was in Presque Isle, Maine. He was sent there on assignment. Everything came back in a rush.

His insides started to twist as he remembered the fight between Deputy Parrish and a man named Rahfey. He remembered the deputy killing the man or whatever he had been. Rahfey had the same weird eyes and long teeth that everyone seemed to have. Like cat people on steroids.

Oh God, none of them had been human, and he'd captured it all on film. Uncharacteristically, his heart began to pound. Usually things didn't freak him out, but something about that situation had him unsettled. He couldn't wrap his mind around the fact that there might be something other than humans in the world.

"Baden won't care what I do. He's going to die anyway." Eric squatted down in front of Devon and leered at him.

Devon found himself starting to laugh. He wasn't sure why. Maybe it was hysteria, but he found the absurdity of the situation amusing. These aliens, or whatever they were, couldn't even agree about whether or not to beat him up. They were just as messed up as humans.

Devon just hoped he was going to live through this.

Eric grabbed the front of Devon's shirt and pulled him close, glaring at him. Eric gave a wicked grin and slowly let his tongue linger over his fangs, making sure that Devon got an eyeful. Something in Devon jumped at the sight of this creature sizing him up for a meal.

"You're going to die here. Understand, human? You are going to die a painfully slow death at my hands. No one will save you. There is no hope of a reprieve. Your life is over."

Devon thrust his head forward as hard as he could and made contact with Eric's. Eric yelped and fell back on his butt, his hand holding his head.

A loud growl filled every space of the cavern as Eric shot back up, but before he could reach Devon, Magnar held him back.

"Bring it, you asshole! You think I'm scared of you?" Devon yelled.

Cree was immediately at Devon's side, attempting to calm him down.

"Please, my brother will kill you," she whispered.

"Brother? You have to be kidding me." He turned to face her and momentarily forgot who he was. She was the most beautiful woman he had ever seen. Her dark eyes were like warm brown velvet, and her lips were full and ruby red. He could see her fangs sticking out below her upper lip. He had to remind himself to breathe.

"Cree! Get away from him this moment!" Eric struggled hard against Magnar, effectively pushing him off. He was suddenly charging toward Devon. Cree stood up and quickly blocked Eric's path.

"Eric, please stop." Her voice barely registered, but it was enough to stop Eric. His face changed and he swallowed. Cree's hands were resting softly against his chest. Devon found himself wishing he were Eric, standing there with Cree's hands on him.

Eric finally nodded, and blood from a small cut on his forehead slowly traveled down the side of his face. "For now. But I will be back." Eric turned and rushed out the cave's opening, Magnar on his heels.

Cree's breath came out in a short burst as she turned to Devon.

"Do not antagonize him, human. He will kill you if you challenge him."

She bent behind him and began to loosen his binding enough that he could wiggle his fingers and get feeling into them.

"Cree's a pretty name," Devon whispered as she stood.

As she looked at him, she smiled, and he thought he had never seen anything more breathtaking. And wasn't that a strange thought as he sat there, preparing to die.

About the Author

After working in the legal and technical fields for many years, Jennifer Osborn took the plunge into full time writing in 2015. She is the award-winning author of The Shilund Saga and The Sentinel's Insurgency. When not writing, she listens to a different muse and creates paintings and collages of all sorts.

She lives in the Cincinnati area with her husband, three dogs and two cats.

Also by Jennifer Osborn

The Sentinel's Insurgency
The Dawning of Scarlett
Torn